HANK HEALS

"David Guy's *Hank Heals* is both a suspenseful story and, for a seeker like me, at once a tantalizing and deeply satisfying experience. The novel's narrator Hank is a sharp-witted credible teller of his tale. I found myself trusting his experience and wisdom. And so reading *Hank Heals* gave me a fresh burst of hope and excitement about the true nature of our beings. It's a rare piece of writing that does that." **—Peggy Payne, author of *Sister India* (a *New York Times* Notable Book) and *Revelation***

"*Hank Heals: A Novel of Miracles* illuminates the depths of religions as diverse as Zen Buddhism and Roman Catholicism, while entertaining readers with an engrossing story full of refreshingly unconventional characters struggling with the possibility of the supernatural. Readers of all spiritual stripes— and secular humanists too—will resonate with and learn from this delightful novel, which is Zen-like in its spare prose and, like the teachings of a Zen master, sparkles with wisdom and wry wit." **—Barbara McHugh, author of *Bride of the Buddha***

"*Hank Heals* is a beautiful book. It's also brilliant, wise, moving, and funny. Like, *really* funny. David Guy's lean prose goes down easy, abounds with classic one-liners, and delivers its spiritual truths casually, like you're shooting the breeze with an old friend. Hank is both totally unique and instantly recognizable as the rough-hewn, warm-hearted, maybe dangerous, probably harmless, definitely bawdy Zen teacher who has nothing to teach and yet amasses a huge following with his healing hands. The story flies along, with its Catholic heart and its Zen wisdom, building to a gorgeously written and touching climax that had me in tears. Spiritual writing like this is rare. David Guy hits the sweet spot between entertaining and enlightening." **—Shozen Jack Haubner, author of *Zen Confidential* and *Single White Monk***

"*Hank Heals* is a novel about Buddhism, Catholicism, meditation, and healing. It's about human relationships, and miracles, and it's about sex. If you want to look into the heart of human longing and finding, this is a book for you." **—James Ishmael Ford, author of *If You're Lucky, Your Heart Will Break***

"*Hank Heals* is a terrific novel written by a deft and effortless storyteller who knows how to keep a yarn moving and immerse you in its characters. We recognize these people: They are us. This is the first novel I have read (well, with the exception of its prequel, *Jake Fades*) about Zen students in contemporary everyday America going about their lives. In the course of the story we learn a lot of real stuff about Zen practice, *zazen* (Zen meditation), and why people need to do it—and, not incidentally, about healing: physically, psychically, spiritually. You will enjoy and learn from this book." **—Norman Fischer, poet, essayist, Zen Buddhist priest, and author of *Selected Poems 1980–2013* and *When You Greet Me I Bow: Notes and Reflections from a Life in Zen***

HANK HEALS

A NOVEL OF MIRACLES

DAVID GUY

Monkfish Book Publishing Company
Rhinebeck, New York

Hank Heals: A Novel of Miracles © 2022 by David Guy

This is a work of fiction. Names, places, characters and incidents are either the product of the author's imagination or are used fictitiously, and any resemblance to any actual persons, living or dead, organizations, events or locales is entirely coincidental.

Paperback ISBN 978-1-948626-76-7
eBook ISBN 978-1-948626-77-4

Library of Congress Cataloging-in-Publication Data

Names: Guy, David, 1948- author.
Title: Hank heals : a novel of miracles / David Guy.
Description: Rhinebeck, New York : Monkfish Book Publishing Company, [2022]
Identifiers: LCCN 2022011890 (print) | LCCN 2022011891 (ebook) | ISBN
    9781948626767 (paperback) | ISBN 9781948626774 (ebook)
Subjects: LCGFT: Novels.
Classification: LCC PS3557.U89 H36 2022 (print) | LCC PS3557.U89 (ebook)
    | DDC 813/.54--dc23
LC record available at https://lccn.loc.gov/2022011890
LC ebook record available at https://lccn.loc.gov/2022011891

Book and cover design by Colin Rolfe
Images used on cover by Francisco Andreotti, Brad West, and Grant Whitty

Monkfish Book Publishing Company
22 East Market Street, Suite 304
Rhinebeck, NY 12572
(845) 876-4861
monkfishpublishing.com

For my teachers
Larry Rosenberg
Josho Pat Phelan
With deep gratitude

Turning away and touching are both wrong
For it is like a mass of fire.
—*Tozan Ryokai, "The Song of the Jewel Mirror Samadhi"*

Everything's Jake.
—*A proverbial expression*

A Note to the Reader

My novel takes place in 2008 and mentions a few Durham, North Carolina, institutions that have since disappeared. I still feel vaguely nostalgic for them. Where do all the bikers go now that Charlie's is gone? (And what were they doing on Ninth Street in the first place?) And Piedmont was once a great restaurant (then not so great). The Green Room seems to survive everything.

In various places in the text, I use italics to indicate that the speaker is speaking Spanish. The English translation is rough, like my knowledge of Spanish (or, as one of my characters would prefer, *Spainish*).

I've lived in Durham for over fifty years, but this is the first novel that I've set here. I'm glad finally to have done so.

Many thanks to everyone at Monkfish Publishing for the wonderful job they've done bringing this book to fruition: Paul Cohen, Susan Piperato, and Colin Rolfe.

PART
ONE

ONE

I came down from early-morning zazen and found Julie Walters in the Whole Foods coffee shop, looking dreadful. She stared straight ahead, her eyes glassy and washed out, seemed to have been crying. The usual gang was sitting over their oatmeal and soy milk; there's quite a crowd of regulars in the morning, but they're a collection of the loneliest, most isolated people on the face of the earth. No one had come over. No one even looked up.

"Julie, honey, what's the matter?" I sat across from her.

Tears poured from her eyes, and her face crumpled. "My cancer came back and I'm going to die," she said.

I knew she'd had cancer. Several years after I went up to study with Jake, a friend called about something else and mentioned she'd been diagnosed. I called her immediately, but by that time she'd had a lumpectomy, rejected any other kind of treatment, and seemed to be on the mend. It hadn't come up as a subject in the years since, seemed a thing of the past.

"You beat it before," I said. "You can beat it again."

"It's a bad sign when cancer comes back in the same breast. It's dreadful."

I'd known Julie quite well in the old days; we'd been sweethearts for three or four months before I went to Maine. She was an emotional woman, but I'd never seen her like this.

Normally she was upbeat. Her reaction to the original diagnosis, years ago, was hardly to blink. That's what made this scary.

"You can beat it, Julie. It doesn't stand a chance with you."

"You mean well, sweetheart. At least you sat down, which is more than anybody else did. But you don't know what you're talking about. I do, unfortunately."

I went over and sat beside her, put my arms around her so she could sob on my shoulder. She really let go, her whole body convulsing. No reason to hold back.

It was true that I didn't know. I'm a nitwit about medical facts.

"Tell me what happened," I said, when she eased up. "Tell me what you know."

"Last week I had a mammogram and there was a bad spot," she said. "After all these years, and checkups all the time, like clockwork. Some of my moron friends wondered why I didn't have the breast removed at the time, just to be safe. But the cancer seemed localized, I'd caught it early, and I'd always loved my breasts. They were my best feature."

I had to concur. Julie in the old days had been one of those Ninth Street sixties people, wore baggy blouses and didn't even own a bra. You saw her breasts wobbling around in there when she moved, saw a nipple sometimes against the fabric, but never saw their shape. It wasn't until her clothes were off that you realized she had huge, beautiful breasts and a knockout figure in general.

Her face was pockmarked from acne when she was a girl, and she often wore large tan glasses that might as well have been a mask. Makeup never touched her face, and she didn't pay much attention to her hair either, which was a nondescript brown and hung halfway down her back. She was nearly six feet, too tall for me, used to buy most of her clothes at the thrift shop, though she'd grown more stylish recently. But I'd never seen a more beautiful body.

"I knew I was taking a risk," she said. "But the life force was strong in me. I believed I would heal."

She was holding a sopping wet handkerchief, sniffling a little, her chest heaving.

"I did heal. I had sixteen years cancer free. But now I get this bad mammogram and it's like hearing the other shoe drop. I don't know what happened."

Tears poured from her eyes again; she collapsed on my shoulder.

"I'm turning your shirt into a snot rag," she said.

"I can wash it."

"I don't know why I even came here. Wanted to be with people. I got the news late yesterday and stayed up all night crying. Had to get out of that house."

That was one of the longstanding mysteries about Julie, the way she always lived alone. She'd had a list of lovers like the Durham phone book, but nobody ever moved in. Not many stayed the night. She had a deeply private side, and that house was her lair.

"I can't stay here," she said. "I'm a mess."

"Stay all you want. It doesn't matter."

"People can't eat. I'm making them sick."

"They always look like that. I don't know what it is with this place."

The regulars never seemed to talk. For a while the store had big tables over near the registers, but they replaced them all with tables for two, which functioned as tables for one. Only singles came in.

And still, not one of them had looked up. They were glued to their laptops.

"It's a good thing you walked in when you did," Julie said. "I was about to slit my throat."

She thought I'd been sent, no doubt. Julie had that side to her.

"Can I touch it?" I said.

"What?"

"Can I touch your breast? Where the spot is?"

I don't know why I said that. I've looked back at that moment endlessly, wondering where that came from—it seems so unlike me—but I can't decide. It was utterly spontaneous.

"Here?" she said. "All these people around?"

"They won't see a thing, I swear. They're afraid to look up."

"It's sweet of you," Julie said.

"It's the right thing. I know it."

I don't know what came over me.

I reached up and cupped her breast.

"It's the other one," she said. "But that does feel good."

I touched her other breast, cupped it in my hand, held it firmly.

"That feels good, Hank. Not to turn away. Not reject it."

"Am I touching the place?"

"You are. It's very small. Right in the middle of your palm."

"It's not the enemy. The spot is not the enemy."

I had no idea where those words came from. What did I know about cancer?

"It's just a form of life," Julie said, "trying to survive."

She touched my hand as it touched her, kissed my cheek.

"I feel your energy," she said. "It's surging all through me. You showed up here for a purpose. You're an angel from God."

It was predictable that she'd think that. It was just like her.

"I can leave now," she said.

Julie was known for her abrupt departures. She'd be deeply passionate in bed, you thought she'd stay for the rest of her life, and two minutes later she'd stand up and put on her clothes.

We scooted over in the booth, stood and hugged.

"Thank you so much, Hank. Thank you for everything."

"You're my girl, Julie. Call when you need me."

"I will." She touched my cheek, walked out.

*

Some years ago, in the eighties, I had a friend who was a political activist in El Salvador during the war, working with the Catholic church. The security forces were terribly repressive, actually murdered people in the streets. In the face of that, nuns and priests held meetings where they read the names of victims and someone would say "*presente*" as each name was read. The person's spirit was present, though the body was gone.

"I think that's the true meaning of resurrection," this woman told me. "Jesus's spirit entered the disciples. It changed them, continued to change them through their lives. He died and they realized Christ. His spirit lived in them."

Not to put too high a tone on things (and I didn't understand that remark at all, when she made it, in the late eighties), but I think a similar thing happened to me after Jake died. It's beyond the fact that he was my teacher and influenced me. It's as if I became larger; I can feel it. I'm starting to act like him as well.

I'd like to think I would always have sat down and comforted Julie, but I know it isn't true. Years before, I would have walked out or wandered to another part of the store. There was something too shutdown about me, too frightened, to open to another's pain. I was like all the other people in the café that morning. Letting her bawl on my shoulder in a public place for minutes at a time, taking out a handkerchief and wiping the tears from her eyes and the snot from her nose, touching her breast in public, saying I knew it was right. It doesn't sound like me. It feels bigger, as if Jake is acting through me.

Someone once asked a famous Zen teacher about compassion, and he said it's the same as reaching behind your back and moving something out of your way when you're half asleep. He meant you don't think about it. You don't wonder how it's done. You *know* how it's done. You're one with the rest of creation, so of course you help out. You'd be stupid not to.

I feel Jake's influence in trivial ways as well. I stand in line for the Whole Foods breakfast and find myself grabbing a muffin instead of wheat toast. I want coffee instead of the tea I always drank. It's all I can do to keep from driving to the Kroger for a box of Krispy Kremes. I always argued with him about the crap he ate. Now he's gone, and I eat it.

I think of how he used to walk, with that silent, bowlegged tread. I think of those meaty, battered hands that he held in the mudra, as if it really did encompass the universe. I think of the quiet smile he wore, not as if something was funny, but because he was delighted to be here.

I find myself doing all those things. I'm actually going bowlegged.

It's three years since he died. I missed him terribly at first, felt rudderless and utterly at sea. The death of my teacher—my second father—also brought back the grief of my real father's death when I was a teenager. I went through that whole round of grief again.

I tried to make a go of it up in Maine, where I had lived with Jake, I really did. I had the house he left me, the job manning the register at a bike shop during the tourist season, a group of students who had been loyal to him. Somehow those things never came together.

It made no sense to run the register when he wasn't repairing bikes. I was just standing there looking out the window most of the time. About half of Jake's students never wanted to study with me, and the other half, discouraged by the sparse attendance, straggled away. A guy named Kevin wanted to work with me but couldn't find a job on Mount Desert to suit him. Jake's daughter Jess kept up with me with copious e-mails and cell phone calls at any time of the day or night, but she was stuck in Cambridge, Massachusetts, and liked her life there.

After a year I made a change. I sold the house and gave half the proceeds to Jess, told her there would be more once I got settled. I moved back to North Carolina and got a job teaching history, an old vocation but one I was good at. I located a room on a second floor just off Ninth Street and opened a zendo, cushions all around and a small altar. I have two periods of sitting and one of walking every morning, starting at 6:00. On Saturday mornings I hold a workshop for people who want instruction.

Mostly, the weekday mornings see me sitting alone. A fair number of people come on Saturdays, but when they drift in during the week and see that it's just me, they don't come back. Some of my high school students thought what I was doing was cool and tried to help, but it's a rare adolescent who can sit for forty minutes, much less get up at 5:00 every day. A few tried gamely during the school year, gave up for the summer.

So I sat alone in that room, which, from a Buddhist perspective, is just as valid. One person sitting is the whole universe. I tried not to think of the past two years as a failure, though a little voice inside kept calling it that. The Zen way is to ignore such voices. You make your best effort and ignore the results.

Jake always told me it took time to get started. You keep sitting, and people appear. The power of sitting draws them.

That day when I saw Julie was a Tuesday in late May, and I spent that whole week sitting alone, and the next one. That second Saturday I was setting up for the workshop—no one had called, but sometimes people came anyway—when I heard the downstairs door open, footsteps coming up. I turned as they got to the top.

"Julie." She looked entirely different. She was beaming.

She walked across the floor and wrapped me in an embrace, held me a long time. Finally she stepped back.

"The spot wasn't there, Hank," she said. "They did an ultrasound and couldn't find a thing. I think your touch opened things up and I was healed. I want to learn what you know. I want you to teach me."

TWO

I've practiced the discipline of Zen for over twenty years, and I know less now than when I started. There's a point where you talk glibly, can go on and on for hours, past that a point where there's nothing to say. The floor goes out from under you and there are no words. I can talk to an old friend like Julie. But at the heart of Zen is a mystery, the same mystery at the heart of life.

Meditation for me has always been essentially physical. I spent years of my life numbing my body, first when my younger brother was born—always a trauma for a middle child—then when my father died, when I was sixteen. I was an emotionally timid person anyway, bound by the various uncertainties of adolescence. That event finished me off.

I couldn't handle the grief and made myself numb. Well into my thirties I walked around like a zombie, with a functioning brain and functioning penis, but no connection between the two (as various women told me). A therapist I saw toward the end of that period tried mightily to help, but even then, I was like a lot of men. I'd heard about feelings. I just didn't know what they were.

I finally discovered them when I sat and watched my body. In Soto Zen, we do nothing with our minds, not a hell of a lot with our bodies, other than put them in a certain posture and try to relax (but the person who discovered that posture, with the body stable like a triangle, right and left sides overlapping, was a genius). The spectacle of a middle-aged body awakening after twenty years of dormancy is something to behold, a fallow field bursting into flowers. The growth just continues. The plants keep changing.

At first I felt incredibly tight, couldn't sit ten minutes without pain. It took months, maybe years, before I could sit comfortably for long periods. (I sometimes think the whole process is learning to relax. The whole process of life is learning to live with a body.) The body did some startling things as it settled. An arm would jump up, fly out to the side. My head would twist on my neck, torso twist practically all the way around. I didn't do these things; they happened. I spent long hours watching the weird machinations of my body.

"Let it go," Jake said. "It knows what it needs."

Once I began to feel the energy—once the body was relaxed—I was stunned. Energy, said the poet and mystic William Blake, is eternal delight, and the man knew what he was talking about. I was astounded by the sheer ecstasy of sitting. "This is better than sex," I thought. "Any sex I ever had."

There's suffering there, of course, trying to maintain such feelings when they happen, thinking they'll happen today because they happened yesterday. But there's a genuine bliss too, that of an infant whose body is free.

"It's called being alive," Jake said. "Welcome to life."

The Buddha spoke of the body within the body, as if there's a perfect body, pure energy, sitting inside this clunky, irregular, arthritic thing we're dragging around. Being in touch with that body—which is there whether we feel it or not—is bliss. Being out of touch is the fallen state the Christians got so worked up about.

They should have shut the hell up and sat for a while. They'd have felt better.

The Japanese speak of the energy center two inches below the navel, the Hara. In Zen we focus on that spot, hold the hands there in a mudra, left over the right, thumb tips touching. We also follow the breath there.

I will admit that, through the years, I felt the energy flow into my hands and wondered if it might be a force for healing. That was a passing fancy as I sat, a thought that moved right through. I never saw myself as a healer. It wasn't an ambition.

Which begs the question: Why did I ask Julie if I could touch her breast?

I did it naturally, the way you reach behind and move something when you're asleep.

"Tell me what the doctor said," I said to her that morning in the zendo.

"He seemed sheepish, quite apologetic. He hadn't meant to scare me, there was definitely a spot on the mammogram, but when they did an ultrasound, which shows more detail, they couldn't find a thing. They looked at it from every angle. There was nothing there."

She looked like a completely different person, as if she'd slept for days. Her skin glowed, her eyes were bright.

"I feel healed, Hank. You unblocked something."

"It doesn't seem possible."

"I felt it at the time, didn't want to say anything. I had my doubts, after all I'd been through. But the energy was stupendous. Much different from the days when you used to, you know, just touch them."

I remembered.

"Massage experts have touched them. Pagan witches in rituals. Healing touchers of all kinds. I've had some of the horniest men in the world touch them, sexual energy coming out their ears. I never felt anything like that. Not even close."

"You don't think it came from you."

"I'd been crying all night, Hank. Praying, screaming, everything I could think of. It was your touch that made the difference. I know it."

So knock me over with a feather.

"Something has caused a profound change in you from the old days," she said. "I couldn't see it before. I didn't really look."

I gave her a brief rundown on my work with Jake. I hadn't caught her up on all that. We hadn't talked at length since I'd been back.

"It's too bad we can't ask Jake about healing," she said. "He'd have lots to say."

"He never said anything before."

"He had to know."

There are stories that the Buddha had extraordinary powers, stories about various practitioners through the years, events which can't be explained. I hadn't heard of many healings.

"All I've got is zazen," I said. "Which is what I was here about in the first place. There was supposed to be a workshop this morning. Nobody showed."

"Have it for me."

Julie had done yoga for years. She could sit full lotus for a while, though she didn't think she could last a whole period. "Five minutes is the most I've done," she said. But half lotus was easy for her, Burmese a breeze. She could also sit back on her heels—what we call *seiza*—like a Japanese. She was as limber as a child.

"When do I do this?" she said.

"First thing in the morning. Last thing at night. Maybe the end of the workday. People do different times. We do it here every morning at six. At least I do. I shouldn't say *we*."

"You can now," she said. "I'll be here on Monday."

"Sounds good," I said. Although I'd heard that before.

"You're my teacher," she said. "I'm so glad I found you."

Hate to say it, but I'd heard that too.

THREE

She was there Monday bright and early, waiting at the door when I arrived. She sat two periods without a hitch, amazing for a beginner. Dead still.

"That's it?" she said.

"Not much excitement."

"It's fine. I'll see you tomorrow."

She gave me a hug and was out the door, another of those Julie Walters exits.

She was there the next morning, and the next. Every day she wore a stretch yoga suit, every day a different color. She didn't look sleepy when she arrived, tired or grumpy, sat in deep silence. Her yoga practice must have been strong.

"There is something else, if you want," I said on Friday.

"I do."

"It's traditional to do chanting after we sit. I haven't because I haven't had regulars. But if you're going to be here, we could start."

"I told you, Hank. I'm your student."

I was starting to believe it.

"You haven't said one word to me," she said. "Am I doing all right?"

"You're great. Like you've been at it for years."

"I want to ask about that."

"Let's do this chanting first."

Normally there's one person ringing bells, also a priest who officiates. The group follows the priest in floor bows and does the chants. I decided we'd do without the priest (who would have been me); I'd ring bells. I showed her how to do the bows; almost immediately hers were more graceful. (Which is not difficult. This arthritis is tough.) We chanted the Heart Sutra, a little rough around the edges. I prompted her with stage whispers.

"Maybe we should try again," she said.

"We'll do it on Monday. There's no hurry."

If she was going to do this, she had the rest of her life.

"That's an interesting document."

"Zen Buddhism in a nutshell."

"Can I take it home?"

"Why not?" I'd made twenty copies of the chant books. A tad optimistic.

This was the first time I'd used one, after a year of sitting.

"So can we talk now?" she said.

"We can. The traditional way is to face each other on cushions. We could also go out for breakfast."

"Let's do the traditional way."

We arranged mats to face each other, and she took her seat. She had beautiful posture, probably better than mine. There was nothing to say.

"So I've been doing yoga," she said. "Used to do classes a lot, now only occasionally. Morning is my time, so I just add this on. Get up a few minutes early."

"Really?"

"Gotten up at five for years. I'm not the dope-smoking, wine-guzzling slut you may remember. Fondly, I hope."

Julie had slept around, but there never seemed anything compulsive or driven about it. She didn't get into emotional angst.

"Anyway," she said. "I've always thought the still yoga poses were the best. And I took this to be a still yoga pose. Forty minutes."

"Right."

"You just stay present. Stay in your body."

"Yes."

"But my mind's going apeshit. In yoga you see patches of mind. But this is like, anything can come up. Yesterday. Things from forty years ago. From when I was three years old."

"You just watch."

"You don't know the extent of this."

"I do, believe me."

"There's nothing I can do?"

"You can try. Most people try. But once you figure out you can't stop it, after fifteen years or something, you come back to this. Sitting and watching."

"It's like I'm not doing anything."

"The more it can seem that way the better."

She was frowning, didn't believe me. Nobody believes it at first.

"Is there a philosophy? Some content?"

"There are things you can read. A ton of stuff, actually. But I don't think Zen is a philosophy. It's something you do."

"There's Taoism in this." She held up the chant book. "I've been into that for years."

"I remember."

Julie's copy of the *I Ching* looked like an old family Bible. Fell open and laid flat at every page.

"It's like you're a monk, or a nun," she said. "Sitting and praying. But what are you praying to?"

"That's what you find out."

Her face was puzzled, the look all new Zen students have.

"You encounter it more purely if you don't have a name for it," I said.

*

Julie's reference to wine guzzling and dope smoking was about a party we both attended twenty-five years ago, one of those old Durham parties, at some ramshackle house near East Campus. I wasn't a partygoer, but my wife Helen had taken Josh to see her parents, so I made a potluck dish and wandered over. Had nothing better to do.

It was a deadly August Durham night, beastly hot and sticky, everybody in shorts and t-shirts. The house didn't have air conditioning, so Julie and I stepped out after we ate. There was a vacant lot next door that housed a vegetable garden, actually three or four gardens, from people all over the neighborhood. Everything was ripe and lush.

Julie was a dyed-in-the-wool Ninth Street person, worked in businesses all over the street, always in retail. She knew everybody, loved to chat. Anyone would have hired her.

We walked out into the pitch black, sweating, me carrying a beer. She had a glass of wine and the last half-inch of a joint. "You'll share this, I hope," she said.

"I'll stick to beer. I had a bad experience once."

"But this is why they call it pot luck."

In Durham, it probably was.

"I've got to pee, actually," I said. "About to burst."

"You can just water the garden. Back where the tomatoes are thick. You won't bother anybody. Come on."

She walked down one of the garden rows.

I had a thing for Julie in those days—she wasn't terribly pretty but was a real sweetheart—but I had a thing for lots of people. There was something wicked and sixties-ish about this whole situation, even if it was the eighties.

We walked down a long row of tomato plants, thick with that summer scent. It was intoxicating.

"Whip it out, Hank," she said when we got way in. "Nobody here but us tomatoes."

I let forth a long, loud stream. She actually tossed the joint into it. It was embarrassing, how long it took.

"Look at that," she said. "The emptier it gets, the bigger."

"Yes."

"That might not fit back into your shorts."

I kissed her. She had a big mouth, sweet with wine, kissed beautifully. She was four inches taller than I, solid and muscular.

She reached down and touched. "Bigger than ever."

"Do you live close to here?"

"I do."

Everybody did. That was our neighborhood in those days.

"Want to go to your place?"

"That would be a possibility. Are you married, Hank?"

"Actually, I am."

"I thought. You have that little boy."

"Right." I looked down.

"Where's the wife tonight?"

"They're away. With her family."

"I see. Hmm." She took a big gulp of wine. "I'm sorry. I'd love to go to my place, under other circumstances. But I don't do that with married men. One of my rules."

"Oh."

"I've been leading you on. Didn't mean to."

"No. It was me."

It was half and half.

"What are we going to do with this?" She looked down at my cock, still in her hand.

"I'll stuff it back in. Just won't go in the house for a while."

"You could, actually. Some women would be all over you."

Somehow the whole thing didn't seem shaming, embarrassing, or rejecting. It was perfectly straightforward.

Four years later I walked into a store where she worked. I went because I knew she was there.

"I'm not married anymore," I said.

"Ah. Good news for me."

＊

I'd never been with anyone quite like her, simultaneously utterly open and devoutly private. She would gladly spend the night with me (though sometimes she abruptly did not do that), but only a couple of times did I stay with her, an extraordinary dispensation.

"I'm not fit company," she said. "Come out of my dreams slowly in the morning, ponder them a lot."

She was not one to cuddle in the morning, and God help you if you suggested anything more.

She was also boldly nonmonogamous, despite her strictures against married men. "Do what you want and I will too," she said. "I don't get into those tangles."

That was perfect for me at the time. I'd been married for years, struggled—not always successfully—to stay faithful, and was ready to sow some wild oats. I'd missed out when I was young.

If I'd been ready to pick one woman, it would have been Julie.

On one occasion I remember actually staying with her, I walked in when she was throwing the *I Ching* in the morning. Tossing some pennies that she always kept on her desk, writing reflections in a journal, a steaming mug of coffee beside her.

"I'm sure you think this is stupid," she said.

"What is it?"

"The *I Ching*? Where were you in the sixties?"

"I was a history buff. Studying the twenties."

"Good Lord."

She showed me how to do it, let me try. "Ask it a question. Don't tell me what. Just hold the question in mind. Ah!" as the pennies spilled out of my hand. "That's a good one."

She didn't need the book. She knew what it said before she looked. Still, she resolutely threw the coins.

"I'm going to continue," she said that morning, after she let me try. "There's coffee in the kitchen. Might be some food around." She wasn't much for breakfast. "You have to amuse yourself, Hank. I'm busy."

It wasn't fun to spend the night at Julie's house. She wasn't available.

She worked retail—often for dreadful salaries—because her real vocation was art, though she was totally dilettantish and half-assed about it, moved from one thing to another. Even when I knew her she was throwing pots for a while, then switched to junk jewelry. She'd been a sculptress, painted in oil, even once sketched a line of clothes.

"I want to be in touch with my creative side," she said. "Doesn't matter how. I like switching around."

"Don't you want to perfect something?" I said. "Make a career?"

"That's why I have jobs, so I won't have to. There's no such thing as perfection, or even particularly good, in my case."

Her ego wasn't in it at all. She just did it.

In more recent years she'd become a body worker; the human body was her work of art. Somehow that was not surprising. It seemed a logical next move.

It was Julie I went to talk to when I decided to study with Jake twenty some years before. I'd met him in Bar Harbor when I was on vacation one summer, taken some classes and started to sit. I'd been fumbling around on my own for a year, trying to do it on my own. I had a feeling my life was out of balance, trusted him.

"This sounds right," she said. "You've got to trust your gut."

"I know it's strange to move up there. It's just for the summer."

"You never know how long it's for." She was right about that.

By the time I got back, at the start of the school year, a woman friend had persuaded her—against all odds—to be faithful, also to be a full-time lesbian. That turned out to be disastrous, eventually, but kept us from getting back together. I kept studying with Jake in the summers, finally moved to Maine to work with him full time. I hadn't had a long conversation with Julie again until that morning in Whole Foods. We'd see each other, stop and chat, nothing more.

✦

She brought flowers for our altar at the zendo and kept it straight. There was an ancient connection between Zen and the arts, and she read up on that. I'd always thought of her as a space cadet, and perhaps for that very reason she wanted to know all the protocol, was terribly particular. Soon she was ringing the bells and I was acting as priest.

"Should you be wearing robes?" she said.

"I could." At least until the real Durham heat kicked in.

"You should."

I started to do that.

"Zazen is like working on art," she said another time. "Except you don't do the art."

Not a bad way to describe it.

"But you're in touch with that energy," she said. "You just watch it. It's fascinating."

"Yes."

"I thought you had to do something to bring that up, like yoga, but you don't. You sit down and it's there."

She sighed, looked out the window.

"That's what you healed me with," she said. "That energy. It's what unblocked me."

About that I had my doubts.

The first weekend after Julie began three people came to the Saturday workshop. The next weekend, five. The next, four more.

"These are friends of yours," I said.

"Some are friends of friends. Who knows if they'll last."

By the end of June I had four people I would have considered regulars. Others sometimes came.

One day in early July the light suddenly dawned. I don't know why it took me so long.

"You told these people I cured you of cancer."

"Not all of them. I don't know all of them. But I told them what happened. You touched me. The spot disappeared."

"Julie."

"It was a major moment in my life. Of course I told people. Not that many. But word gets around."

Jesus Christ. So to speak.

"They're not expecting you to walk on water, Hank. But you did this thing. You've got to get used to it."

How could I possibly get used to that?

FOUR

It was the last week of June when one of the regulars approached me, a little woman named Margaret. People called her Meg.

"Julia said it was. like, possible to sit down and talk. Get some help with all this."

"Sure."

I hadn't made a big deal of *dokusan*—the private meeting between teacher and student. I was still getting used to having a group. The whole thing snuck up on me.

"Thursday's my day off. Would that be okay? After service?"

"Great."

Meg was a cook at Elmo's, worked the second shift. If I went in there for lunch she'd come out and give me free coffee. Try to give me a piece of pie.

Jake would have loved a student who gave him pie.

By that time we almost looked like a Zen group. Julie had taken the role of *doan*. I entered the zendo in my robes promptly at 6:00, offered incense, and she rang three bells. We sat a forty-minute period, walked ten, sat for thirty minutes. After that we did a short service, Julie ringing bells and me acting as *doshi*. She picked things up quickly.

We had the four regulars at that point, five or six others who came occasionally. After service we cleared things up and put the cushions away. The room was a dance studio the rest of the day. I arrived early to set things up and create a little altar. Julie brought in flowers.

On Thursday Meg and I arranged the cushions to talk in the middle of the room. The dancers didn't arrive until 8:30, so we had plenty of time.

She was tiny; that was the first thing I would have said. Not five feet, with small hands and a narrow face. She had a unique haircut, shaved close on one side, hanging down long on the other, so her bangs curved around and covered her left eye. She couldn't see out of it, it seemed. I would have thought that annoyed her. It annoyed me, though I couldn't do much about it. Beautiful auburn hair, but only half a head of it.

She had a small mock diamond on one side of her nose. Her only jewelry.

Her posture wasn't exemplary, like Julie's, but it was all right. I hadn't made a huge deal out of posture (though the Japanese did). I'd get to it if people stuck around.

Meg's torso was so small I could hardly tell if it was straight or not.

"I met Jule at, like, an art class years ago," she said. "Known her all that time. Now she's my bodyworker. We were lovers for a while. Before that. She doesn't mix, like, business and pleasure. Except that her business is a huge pleasure."

Julie wouldn't let a customer be a lover. She had told me.

"Said you two used to be lovers, years ago. Before all this."

I nodded.

No telling what Julie had told these folks.

"Is it okay if we just, like, talk? I don't know how to do this."

"It's good to talk about your life a little."

Though I didn't need to know every single lover.

"Jule says you cured her of cancer. Touched her tit and zapped the hell out of the cells. *That's* pretty cool."

Shit. "I did touch her breast. The spot from her mammogram disappeared. That's all we know."

"She *said* you wouldn't take credit for it."

This wasn't how I'd envisioned beginning.

"How old are you, Meg?"

"Twenty-eight. No, wait. Twenty-nine."

She'd known Julie for years, she said. The woman was robbing the cradle.

I'd have to get on her about that.

"What brought you to practice?" I said.

"Other than the fact that you're Jesus Christ?" She grinned. "I'm kidding, Hank. Lighten up."

I hadn't seen Meg smile before. Didn't know she could.

What I really wanted to do was lean forward and move that hair away from her eye. It was as if she were sighting me through a telescope.

"The thing is, like, it's kind of embarrassing, though Jule said you wouldn't mind. I got this thing about, like, picking guys up at bars. Doing it with strangers."

This little girl went to bars?

She looked all of about fourteen.

"Not total strangers. After a while you know the guys. But random people. Total slut behavior."

"Where?"

"Charlie's. The Green Room."

"You shoot pool?"

"I'm a crack shooter, since I was a kid. I could be a hustler, if I wasn't a hustler the other way. Not that I exactly take money."

"Meaning what?"

"They lose the game. Pay up. Then I wind up going home with them."

The fascinating thing about this conversation was that it was so matter of fact. She wasn't even blushing.

"I hope you're careful."

"I'm a walking condom dispenser. Never depend on the guy."

"But those men at Charlie's." It had become a biker bar. Long row of motorcycles on weekends.

"They're like the Green Room. Some of the same guys, actually. Look mean, but they're just the old boys from high school. They like me because I look young."

I'd never see Charlie's the same way again. They had outdoor tables, and it always just looked like a bunch of middle-aged men. Drunks, of course.

"So what's the problem? You like them and they like you."

"It's hard to describe. I get home late at night. Had a long day at work. I like shooting pool. It relaxes me. And it's a major source of income. But I have this restlessness. Like I've got to get out of the house. Got to have sex."

That I could relate to.

"I've gone to shoot pool, maybe have a couple beers. And I wind up with some guy every night. More beer. Whiskey. Cocaine."

Jesus.

"I want to do it and then again, I don't. Can't figure the whole thing out."

"You didn't pick Julie up at the Green Room."

"She was my one thing with a woman. This older, wiser soul. But I'm not really a dyke. Not that she is."

There was no categorizing Julie.

"This thing with the guys is different."

For sure.

In a way, I was sitting there talking to myself. Jake said that would happen sooner or later.

"Jule thought this sitting might help. And it's been great. Getting up, being here. Keeps me out of trouble. But I've still got that itch at night, that restlessness. Almost went out a couple times this week."

"But then you didn't."

"I'm holding it off, being a good girl. But I can't forever."

Sex when you're young seems overwhelmingly physical. Actually, in my experience, it was largely a matter of the mind. It wasn't her body putting her through all that, though it might have felt that way.

Sitting breaks down the compulsion. You feel the physical part as energy, see the mental part as thoughts. Then you can make some choices. You won't always make the right ones. But you see the impulse clearly.

Unfortunately, for me, that took years.

I explained all that to Meg, didn't name a timeframe. Might be quicker for a woman. But it isn't easy.

"It doesn't help until *you* see it," I said. "Doesn't help for me to say it."

"It helps a little."

"It's not a quick fix. You might screw up sometimes. Don't be hard on yourself."

"I think I'll be screwing up soon. I have a feeling."

"The important thing is to keep sitting. Make that a practice for life. And try to bring the practice with you. Be mindful when you go to these places, when you go home with somebody. See the impulse when it arises. See if it's suffering. Don't assume that."

"I thought maybe you could touch me."

"What?"

"The way you did Jule. You have this energy, she says."

"Meg...."

"She has it too. The bodywork is healing. She says I need to feel things more deeply."

"That's what this practice does."

"I even thought, I don't want to say the wrong thing, but I thought you could fuck me. Show me the real thing."

Good Lord. "It wouldn't be any more real."

"I read about this Indian guy, Muktananda. Used to put it in soft, then stand there talking to the girl. People called it abuse. The girls were kind of young, but they said it was wonderful."

He was picked up for assault with a dead weapon.

"We all have the healing energy inside us," I said. "It's not a special thing. It's a human thing."

"It doesn't show up for everybody."

"Over time, as you sit, you'll feel it. That's the healing."

"Then how come people can't touch themselves? How come Jule couldn't zap her own tit?"

"I don't know. I don't understand."

"If you hadn't touched her she'd be dying. I wish we could try."

"If I thought it was right, I would. But this is the right thing, I'm sure. Keep sitting. Tap the energy."

"That assumes I can keep it up."

That was the question. I couldn't answer that one.

Meg did a little bow. She got up and headed out the door. "Thanks anyway, *Sensei*."

"Call me Hank." Where the hell did she get that?

I walked to Whole Foods and Julie was sitting at the booth where I'd found her that first morning. We'd taken to going there after the morning sit. We liked the food, and it was a good place to talk. Julie was eating scrambled eggs and a muffin.

She looked like a new person, of course, ever since she'd been coming to the zendo. Bright and cheerful, relaxed and rested. She'd been reprieved from a death sentence. In her opinion.

"Where did Meg get the idea of calling me *sensei*?" I said.

"I've been reading up. That's what people call their teachers, right?"

"I called mine Jake."

"What did he call his teacher? In Japan?"

"How would I know? Listen. Where did she get the idea I should touch her?"

"Not from me. I told her my experience. I've told lots of people."

"How many?"

"I don't know. Most of my clients. Some friends." She was blushing.

"The thing I have to teach people is zazen. You understand that, right?"

"I do."

"And it's not really teaching. It's a few words of instruction. They learn on their own. My job, my only job, is to keep them at it."

"I don't think you understand you have a gift. A special gift."

"I don't know a thing about that."

"*I* know." Julie stared at me.

That was the crux of the matter. Julie believed something about me that I didn't believe myself.

"If I had that gift I'd use it," she said. "Selectively. People need healing."

"Touching Meg isn't going to make her stop having sex with random men."

"It made me feel different. Made me act different."

"Much less screwing her. Which she also suggested."

"Oh God." She laughed. "She's been reading the Internet."

"Everybody wants a quick fix. There is no quick fix."

"I know. But there is such a thing as touching people and helping them. I believe that. I make a living at it."

I didn't have her confidence. I was scared of it.

"You need to be open to what you have," Julie said.

FIVE

The next person to show up for dokusan—about a week later—was a woman named Dana. She'd come to the introductory workshop one Saturday with four other women, all of whom had since disappeared, but Dana kept coming. She hadn't said boo to me the whole time, barely hello or goodbye. Yet here she was with her tiny voice, almost a whisper, asking if she could "do dokusan." She actually used the word.

She was another Julie disciple, a bodywork client. Maybe I should have turned the group over to Julie. Dana had jet black hair with bangs in front; it hung past her shoulders in back. She was extremely pale, plump and soft, had a light mustache above her upper lip. Now that she'd gotten there and was sitting in front of me, she seemed to wish she were anywhere else. She couldn't meet my eyes. The first thing I noticed—though, as I've said, I'm not a fanatic—was her posture.

"You're slumping a little, sweetheart."

Sweetheart? Where the hell did that come from?

That wasn't the word she noticed. "Slumping?"

"Your back's rounded, your shoulders hunched. Your head looks down. It brings your whole body forward."

"So I'm not doing it right."

"It's not a matter of right or wrong. Just helpful to open up. Let the energy flow."

"That's my whole problem." Tears started to flow, pouring from her eyes. She leaned forward even further. She didn't sob, quite, but started to sniffle.

Your temptation is to comfort the person, but this is dokusan after all, and anyway it's best to let her cry her own tears. You can't cry them for her.

"I knew I'd cry," she said. "I always do."

"Everybody cries. It doesn't matter." Definitely wasn't the first time. "Julie tells me you're a musician."

"I try to be. Would like to."

"She said you trained in Boston. Have a rich background. You've been playing since you were a child."

"I'm a clerk in a music store. I sell banjos to children."

That seemed, as she said it, to be the most shameful fact in the world. She might as well have told me she sold them porn.

"They need banjos," I said. "Everybody should have one."

If she wanted to fall to pieces, that was her business. I hadn't heard anything tragic yet. Julie had clued me in on what was coming.

Hell, I'd wanted to be Jacques Barzun, and here I was teaching high school history.

"I hoped to be a concert musician. Play with an orchestra, small ensembles. I was told all through my childhood that I had a gift. And I got into Berklee. You don't just waltz in there."

So to speak.

"You must be very talented."

"I no sooner got enrolled than I started choking up. Had a chance to get an audition, give a recital, and I'd be terrible. All kinds of mistakes."

"Ones I could have heard?"

"My teachers knew. *I* knew."

The weird thing about this whole thing was her voice. It was tiny, far away, lost. You might have thought she'd work herself into a rage, at least at herself.

"I got to a point where I couldn't do it at all. Couldn't go out there."

"When was that?"

"Four years ago. I dropped out. Moved away. Eventually moved down here."

I wondered how many people she'd told this story to. She seemed to have it down.

"I was also in love with my professor," she said.

"What was he like?"

"It was a she."

"Oh."

"Notorious for seducing students. All her little girls. But she never made a move toward me. One time I heard her in her office, she didn't know I was next door. 'Dana's such a little lump,' she said."

Not a bad description, actually.

"*That's* what she thought of me."

"It's not who you are." It probably was how she was acting at the time.

"I was shattered when I moved here, back home for me. Quite a comedown. I thought I'd at least be able to make a life. I'm not a culture snob. I like pop, country. Thought it would help to get away from the concert hall."

"That sounds right."

"But I'd get together with folks. Bluegrass bands. A little jazz group. They'd have all these ideas. Immediately I'd start finding fault. This wasn't right, that wouldn't work. It wasn't anything about the group. It was me. I was terrified I couldn't do it. I'd find some way to back out."

It was amazing, the self-knowledge that woman had. She had the whole thing figured out in her head. Hadn't done her a damn bit of good.

The problem was in her body. She was tied up in knots.

"I know I have music in me," she said. "I can feel it welling up, all the time. Just can't get to it."

She was burning with rage, was the truth of the matter. She should have torn the room apart. But she sat there speaking in that tiny voice.

"I want you to touch me," she said.

Here we go again.

"Julie says an enormous energy pours from your hands. It shot through her whole body, burned away cancer as if it didn't exist. If you touched me that way it might unleash my creativity, free the power that's in me. I know it."

The whole time she was talking—pardon the comparison—I was thinking about a story from the Gospels, the paralyzed man who lay beside a pool that supposedly had healing powers. The story was that when the wind passed over the waters, the first person in would be healed. It was a beautiful story, but the guy waiting there was paralyzed. He could never be the first in. It was a hopeless situation. As hopeless as Dana thinking I could unleash her creativity.

It's told as a healing story. *Take up your pallet and walk.* But I think Jesus was telling the guy to take charge of his life. Quit sitting there in a hopeless situation. He had paralyzed himself, lying there looking for pity.

"There's no telling what happened with Julie's cancer," I said.

"That's what you say. She's quite clear about it."

"It's wonderful that it's gone. But the healing was in her."

"You brought it out."

In an odd way I was tempted. Dana had what she needed to make herself whole. If she thought my touch would bring it out, maybe it would.

I couldn't give in to that.

If I'm convinced of one thing about the Buddha, it's that he believed in our power to take care of ourselves. When he was a young yoga student and met masters of meditation, his response wasn't to see them as holy men. He respected them, knew he could learn from them. But his deepest response was: I have the same capacities they do. I can do what they did.

When students asked how they would know whether to accept a teaching or not, he gave a long list of reasons not to. He didn't want them to accept it even because *he* had said it. When you know for yourselves it's true, he said, when you know by your own experience, then accept it. He didn't ask them to take anything on faith.

And when he died and his students feared losing him, wondered who would lead, he said: Be a lamp unto yourselves. He had an infinite belief in our own human capacity. That was what he taught, not that we should worship somebody.

Dana was locked up with fear. An anxiety arose when she tried to play music and robbed her of energy. She tried to fend anxiety off, hold it at bay, and that soaked up more. The power of anxiety was enormous, as was the energy to hold it off. The struggle left her pale, lifeless, speaking with this tiny voice.

What she had to do—though it goes against our every instinct—was to let the anxiety pour through her. She'd no longer be fighting anxiety with energy—would no longer be at war with herself—and could use that energy for herself. She'd be a different person.

That was what she needed, not a touch from me.

"What you're saying sounds true," she said, when I told all that to her. "Makes sense at some level. But it's hard."

"It's a long-term change. A way of dealing with experience."

"What's it have to do with sitting?"

"You learn it in sitting, with small things. And if you go on a long retreat, you'll deal with deeper and deeper levels. If fear is your thing, fear will come up."

"I'd like it to, kind of, just happen. Thought you could jump-start me."

"That's a dream. Buddhist practice is real."

Dana had come for a miracle but took in the truth of what I said. It always helps to come in touch with reality. It has a certain feel, solid, like the earth. She'd also had someone listen to her. She looked relieved as we gathered the cushions and put them away.

Then I blew it. Jake was always a big hugger, with all his students; it was the Jewish mother in him. It was part of what we did with everybody; I'd never thought about it. And Dana was such a sad sack, needed bucking up. I gave her a hug before we walked out.

"Oh!" She almost screamed. "Oh!" She burst into tears again, sobbing against my shoulder. "That was it. That was so what I needed. Thank you, Hank. God. Thank you."

I must have stood there for five minutes holding her while she sobbed. She was so soft, also terribly slight. There was nothing to her.

By the time she walked down the stairs and out on the street, she was glowing.

I was not. I walked across the street to the café.

"You might as well accept it," Julie said. "There's something about your hands."

"It's all in their minds."

"It wasn't in my mind."

"What I told her was right. She needs to meet her fear."

"There's such a thing as using your touch to help people. It supplements what you tell them. Jesus did it."

"Julie, please."

"It can add to what you say."

I shook my head. What was I going to do for the rest of my life, not touch people?

"This can be a good thing Hank, believe me."

"Nothing can be good if people think I have that power and they don't."

SIX

Julie lived in a rental house on Iredell, one of those pale-yellow places that—so the rumor went—were all owned by one guy; that's how you knew he owned them, by the color. I walked over on a godawful hot afternoon a couple of days after I saw Dana. I was wearing a t-shirt and some cut-off jeans, a pair of sandals, but was dripping sweat by the time I got there. I love the intensity of those Durham summer days.

I was going over to have Julie convince me about the healing power of touch.

"You don't know a thing about it," she had told me. "Other than having it, in spades. I make a living at it."

"I'm sure you know more."

"It isn't really knowing. There's a whole body of knowledge about giving a massage, all the physiological stuff. But there's a kind of knowing that exists in the body, quite beyond that technique. You feel your way with your hands. Some people have it and some don't."

"Why, if you have it, can't you heal yourself?" I was taking a page from Meg.

"I tried, believe me. Tried everything."

"Maybe you did heal yourself. It was you."

Julie shook her head.

"I know the healing took place when you touched me. I felt it. I don't know why, I admit. But I know it happened."

Where did that leave me? Not having any idea what I'd done, how I'd done it.

"It's something about two people coming together," Julie said. "One giving the other what she doesn't have. Maybe never can have, for herself."

That made sense.

"It's energy," Julie said. "But it comes from outside. Have you had a massage?"

"Lots of times, years ago. All-Girl Staff."

"Not that."

"I've had a few. Not since I've been sitting."

"You ought to let me work on you."

Hence my trip to that yellow house on that blazing afternoon, dripping with humidity. I'd been to the Y and had my swim, was already relaxed. My appointment was for 5:00. Julie opened the door in a white cotton blouse and billowy pants, the lightest possible fabric. I had taken a step inside when I noticed the obvious, also the almost unbelievable, for Durham.

"You don't have air conditioning."

"I have an attic fan for nighttime. Ceiling fans in every room, great circulation. I hate air conditioning, to be honest. Hate that fake air."

"I'm not wild about it. But this kind of day."

"For massage, as far as I'm concerned, it can't be too hot. A steam room would be fine."

A steam room was what we had.

Julie's place was suitably Julie, minimal furniture, lots of artwork. There was a large living room up front, two bedrooms and a bathroom in the middle, a kitchen and eating nook all the way back. The whole place was cluttered with pottery, hanging art, mobiles, wire sculptures; at the same time, it was extremely neat, beautifully arranged. The massage room was the smaller bedroom, basically just the table with sheets on it, a small corner table with oils, a music system playing Chinese restaurant music. I love that stuff. Only wish I could sing along.

She had me lie face down first, my face in a head rest. I was slick with sweat, but that didn't seem to matter. It mixed with the oil.

"As much as possible," she said, "as I say to all my clients, I want you to put your mind into your body, right where my hands are. You ought to be good at that."

"No better than anyone else."

"Let your thoughts go, feel your energy. We won't talk."

I'd had a few massages in the old days. God knows enough women had put their hands on me. It wasn't just that Julie was expert in what she did, though she was. There was something about her hands, a feeling to them other people didn't have. It was apparent from the start. She had power, a certain energy. She could have touched me anywhere.

I conked out a couple of times. One time, on my back, I snored so loudly I woke myself up. The experience in general was extraordinarily soporific. I should have had her over before bedtime.

I hadn't realized she'd be touching my belly. Maybe I just hadn't realized how intimate that would be. She rolled the sheet way down, gently—but deeply—touched me there. Out of nowhere, I started to cry.

"I don't know what this is," I said.

"It doesn't matter."

I had a good long cry, really sobbing. She didn't stop with her hands. There was no content at all. I felt sad, but not about anything specific.

"There's often sadness in the belly," Julie said.

I was totally zonked out after I cried. Deeply relaxed. I'd been lying with my eyes closed because it seemed comfortable, but at that point I'm not sure I could have opened them. Julie finished up with my shoulders and neck. At one point she dug her fingers into the base of my skull, so my head was propped up just slightly, and let me lie like that a long time. My body was dead still.

After that, she had finished, or so I thought, still seemed to be hovering around. Then I felt a tingling at the base of my spine, a strong blissful sensation, radiating through my body, up and down. It felt like energy, felt like love: I'd never felt anything like it. I hadn't had a sexual thought through the whole massage, wasn't having one now, but the energy gave me an erection.

"What's this?" I still hadn't opened my eyes.

"I'm balancing your chakras with a crystal," she said. "Yours seem balanced."

She didn't say anything for a few moments, then, "What's your romantic life like these days?"

"Nonexistent."

"I was wondering."

"But this...." I knew the sheet was poking up. "It isn't about romance," I said. "It's much more primal. Pure energy."

"Yes."

"I've never felt anything like it."

"I have."

I still hadn't opened my eyes.

Julie drew down the sheet, climbed up on the table, and blew me.

I should mention—perhaps should have mentioned earlier—that that was her favorite sexual act. Intercourse came in a distant second. She had a large mouth, could relax it easily, and blow jobs were effortless for her. She had loved taking care of me.

After she finished she lay on top of me for a while, and I held her, then she walked out, and I got dressed. When I came into the living room, she had poured glasses of lemonade, was sitting on the couch. I sat across from her.

She wasn't smiling. I'd never seen Julie nervous before.

"I don't want that to change things," she said. "I don't know what came over me."

"Sure."

It would have seemed just as right to walk away and do nothing. It didn't matter.

"It was as if we'd already made love," I said. "Whether you did it or not."

"I felt this huge sense of love in the room. Not for you, especially. Just love."

"Yes."

"Though I do love you, Hank. I love you."

"I love you too."

"But I don't want this to be a love affair. As nice as that might be. I need you as a teacher."

"I know."

"That's more important."

I knew what it was to need a teacher. To have a feeling that you absolutely had to have one, that finding the right one was a precious thing. Much more rare than romantic love.

Julie and I hadn't done dokusan again, but we'd had breakfast almost every day, talked endlessly about practice. I told her stories about Jake, stories he'd told me about his teacher. She soaked up everything I said.

"I didn't realize I was looking for something," she said. "I'd given up so long ago that I didn't know I was still looking. It's like you finally decide you don't have a home, there isn't a place in the world for you, then you stumble across it."

"Yes."

"We could ruin that with a love affair. Blow the whole thing."

Not the best choice of words, perhaps.

"You always had that thing for sex," she said.

"I did."

"But you're over that."

"You're never over it."

"That's what worries me."

"I can handle this, that it happened. Won't fixate on it." At least not that she would see. "I understand how sacred the bond is, with your teacher."

"It wasn't an impulse. I knew what I was doing. I didn't get worried until afterwards."

It was a loving moment that was beyond romantic love, much larger than that.

"So why don't you have a love life?" Julie said.

"Haven't found the right person, as they say."

"There are right people all over the place."

"I'm still ambivalent about the whole thing. The way it used to take me over. All the problems I had. Staying alone seems simpler."

"What do you do about sex?"

"What any single person does."

Julie had always been a fierce proponent of masturbation. Even back when she had all the lovers, she saw it as the primal sexual act, out of which all the others emerged. No number of other lovers took her away from her lifelong affair with herself.

"There are women who would be pounding at your door if they knew."

"Let them pound."

I'd be pounding on something else.

I'd finished my lemonade, and she'd poured me another glass. She glanced at her watch.

"I have another client coming."

"I didn't know." I took a long swallow from my glass.

44

"Evenings are busy. It's when people can come. So what do you think of the power of touch now?"

"More bewildering than ever."

"But it's powerful."

"Definitely. Does that often happen, with the crystal?"

"I've never seen it before. Men get a hard on, but not from the crystal."

"And what do you do?"

"Not that. That's a no-no in this business."

"Your secret is good with me."

"It's all one energy, I think. Sexual. Spiritual. What people call healing. They make these distinctions. But it's all one thing."

"I know."

"It's all healing, if you use it the right way."

SEVEN

It was a week or so after I'd had that massage from Julie, and I'd just stepped out of the downtown Y, wondering what to do for dinner. I love that moment on a summer evening. The air is deadly hot, and still. Billowing clouds hang low in the sky, looking like rain, but never quite pull the trigger. I was relaxed from my swim, feeling slightly drained, and the heat enveloped me. I used to get worn-out by heat, but as I get older I can't get enough. Especially at the end of the day, when the sun isn't bearing down.

I was standing there feeling it when a guy stepped up to me.

"You're Hank, aren't you?" he said. "I'm a friend of Julie's. Stone Rockwell."

I don't know what came over me. I don't usually make smart remarks to strangers.

"What a name," I said. "Your parents must have been brilliant." Or had a sense of humor. Something.

"Actually, I was brilliant. Gave myself that name back in the seventies, when everybody was changing names. I lived in Chapel Hill."

That explained a lot.

"Better than Edgar Steigerwalt, don't you think?"

"Might be."

"For bodywork. Wanted to sound solid, somehow. But it

was also the seventies, what the hell. I wanted to sound hard. Rock well."

Maybe he wasn't so brilliant.

"Do you have a minute?" he said.

"Sure."

"I've been wanting to look you up. This is serendipity." Or so they say in Chapel Hill. "Can I buy you a beer?"

"Weren't you going in the Y?" He carried a gym bag.

"I can do that anytime. Why don't we go over to Piedmont?"

It was one of those new Durham restaurants, just across the street.

I had seen Stone at the Y on various occasions. He was a memorable figure, mostly bald, with a shiny dome of a skull, but what hair he had—around the fringes—grew long and hung to his shoulders, a bright blond. He had a ravaged face, major craters under his eyes, and a massive belly, which he concealed with dashiki-type shirts like the one he had on now. He walked the treadmill at a moderate pace, sweating profusely, snorting like a horse, gazing around as if someone should rescue him from this ordeal. He seemed engaged in a losing battle with that belly.

"They have a wonderful wheat beer here," he said as we stepped into Piedmont. "I love a wheat in the summer. Often stop in after my workout."

Apparently so.

"I'd rather have something dark." I hate wheat beer.

Maybe I should have told him I was sensitive to wheat. Chapel Hill guys understand that.

Stone put in an order and slapped down a twenty. They brought me a stout, black as pitch. It tasted great.

Piedmont was a bit upscale for my taste; I hadn't been there. They had just a small bar, seven or eight stools. The place wasn't crowded. It was early for dinner.

"You look tense, Hank." Stone took a major slug from his beer. "Have you been stressed?"

"Not that I know of." Maybe I was stressed because he had showed up.

"Here." He reached up to my collarbone, pressed with a thumb on one side, fingers to the other. "Better?"

"As a matter of fact, yes." It felt great. Not that there was anything wrong in the first place.

"You might want to let me work on you sometime. I went to massage school with Julie. Do a wonderful full body."

"I bet."

"I exchange with Julie now and then. She told me you'd been over."

I hope she didn't tell him how we finished up.

I'd have Stone skip that.

He eased up on my shoulder, took a major hit from his beer.

"She told me about the extraordinary healing you did for her. I was deeply moved."

I was going to have to tell Julie to quit talking about that, however extraordinary it was. This was getting out of hand.

"I'm not at all sure it happened," I said.

"She's quite convinced."

"It could have been a mistaken diagnosis. Pure coincidence."

"You can't fake the energy. Julie felt it."

"Julie has energy too."

"I wish you could teach me. Is it some kind of Daoist thing? Reiki?"

"It was just my hands."

"Of course it was your hands. But it came from somewhere. If you could give me some pointers on that."

I had no idea what he wanted from me.

"I have people coming to me every day. Fibromyalgia. Chemical sensitivities. Lyme disease. Chronic fatigue. Made ill by the toxic world we've created."

He definitely practiced in Chapel Hill.

"They cry out for a healer. I could be that man."

That sounded like a stretch.

"I have the technique. Studied with the best teachers in Asheville. But I don't have those magic hands. Where do they come from?"

"I can't imagine."

"People have been studying energetic touch for centuries. Millennia. You don't just stumble into it."

"I don't know where it came from."

"You could come work with me. Touch selected clients."

"I have no training."

"There is no training for what you've got. That's my whole problem."

I was beginning to wish I'd never touched Julie's breast. Or at least that she'd never told anybody.

"You could sit zazen with us," I said. "There's always that."

"I could never sit zazen. Christ!" He drained his glass, gestured to the bartender.

Lots of people say that, but I don't believe it. They haven't tried.

"You ready?" he said, when the bartender stepped up.

Not quite. I had taken only one sip of my beer.

I *was* ready to get out of there.

"I do know one thing," Stone said. "You have a gift." He turned his ravaged gaze on me. "And there's money to be made on this. Big money."

*

"Stone's always been nuts," Julie said. "How'd you run into him?"

"He nabbed me coming out of the Y. I was an innocent bystander."

I had stopped at Julie's on the way home. I had to talk to her. She was putting sheets on the massage table, setting up for a client.

"I knew him years ago," she said, "when I first got into this. He was trim, good looking. Had a full head of blond hair, wore it long. He looked like a Viking."

Or a professional wrestler.

"I think that belly of his, which is gargantuan, is all beer," she said.

"I don't doubt it." He'd ordered a third pint before I managed to get out of there, pleading another appointment. Didn't look like he'd be working out that day.

"I thought this would be a good day job," she said. "Fit in with the other things I did. But I always thought Stone was one of those guys who just wanted to get his hands on people. You run into such creatures at massage school. He was all over you, all the time. There was something creepy about it."

You're telling me.

"He saw it as a way to get laid, basically."

"I thought that didn't go on."

"It's not supposed to."

"We're talking men or women here?"

"Both, is my impression. He just had those wandering hands."

"He said you two exchange massages."

"That's an exaggeration. He'll call me now and then. I pick up things from him. He's a good technician. The whole sex thing has died down. It's been twenty-five years."

"He says he wants to heal the world. Cure Chapel Hill of chemical sensitivities." A gargantuan task if there ever was one.

"He's always had that too. A messiah complex. He does talking therapy along with massages, pries into all your problems. 'You're tight here. Must be your heart chakra.' Stuff like that. Always telling people they look stressed."

Shit.

"Nobody looks more stressed than he does," she said. "All the time. He just tries too hard, doing a million things at once. He'd be better off sticking with massage."

This was the kind of person she was spilling the beans to.

"I wish you hadn't told him about your supposed healing," I said.

She had finished with the table, turned to me.

"That was bad judgment. It was the day I'd actually seen the doctor, found out I was okay. I had an appointment to massage Stone. He was moved by what I told him. He started crying."

God knows how many bars he'd told the story in since.

"Said you were the kind of healer he'd always wanted to be."

Good grief.

There was a knock on the screen door.

"That's my six o'clock," Julie said.

"I better get out of here."

"You don't need to. It's Meg."

We stepped into the living room as the young lady came in the door. She was wearing jeans and a ragged t-shirt, her little nipples poking through. Her hair hung over her eye in that annoying way, and that eye was closed as well. Her head seemed to lean in that direction, so her hair hung down more, and her face was deadly pale. She seemed to be squinting against the light, but there wasn't much to speak of. She was just squinting.

She hadn't been to the zendo for three days. I'd wondered what was up.

"Hank," she said. "I didn't know you were here. Hope I'm not interrupting."

"I just stopped in to talk."

"You two aren't getting back together?"

Somehow Meg was fascinated at the thought of our past romance, asked about it all the time.

"No."

Nothing going on, other than the occasional blow job.

"You look terrible, baby," Julie said. "What's wrong?"

"Headaches, for almost a week. Haven't been to work in days. I'm like, dying."

"You look it."

"I haven't known what to do. Didn't know if I should cancel."

"No. Massage can help."

"I feel like I'm about to throw up. Rather not do that in front of my teacher here."

She looked at me through her one open eye.

All my life, for whatever reason, headache is the pain I've been most sympathetic to. My younger brother had terrible headaches when he was young, and I hated to see him go through that, pain in the ass though he often was. He was this little kid with a huge head, would sit there looking miserable. "I've got to do something about these headaches," he'd say, like a middle-aged business executive. I hated feeling helpless beside him.

Again—as I had with Julie, though I asked her first—I reached out my hand to touch Meg's head. I touched the place where her hair hung over, where her eye was closed. "Oh, Jesus," she said. I reached out with my left and put it on her neck, as if to steady her. Her body started to shake. "God!" she said. "God." She was shaking so hard I thought she might fall down. She kept shaking and shaking, like nervous shudders. Finally she gave one last shudder, opened her eyes as if startled, and threw up, right between us. She leaned way down, so it didn't do much damage. Spattered our sandals a little. She really got it out.

"God," she said. "Hank. I'm so sorry."

"Don't be," I said. "You can't help it."

"I'll get a mop," Julie said. "Stay right there."

She came back with a mop and bucket, a towel to wipe off our feet. Got everything up in no time.

"This is so embarrassing," Meg said.

"It's happened before," Julie said. "Headaches do that."

"I bet you feel better," I said.

"The headache's gone," Meg said. "That did it."

"You felt the energy," Julie said.

"Big time. It was amazing."

"I told you," Julie said. "I've been telling everybody."

"I believe it. I believed it all along."

"Why did you touch her, Hank? When you won't touch anyone else."

"I don't know. I just saw the pain."

"There's pain everywhere. Don't you see it?"

"Jesus, Hank." Meg stepped over and hugged me, that little body pressed against my torso. "You don't know what you've got there. It's like a jolt of electricity."

"That's what I've been saying," Julie said.

"You want to fuck sometime?" Meg said. "I mean, seriously."

"It's not for trivial things," Julie said.

"How's that trivial?" Meg said.

"You can help people," Julie said to me. "You can really help people. There's the proof right there."

I didn't know what I'd done. I definitely didn't know how I felt about it.

"Why don't we have some of that lemonade," I said.

"Definitely," Meg said. "I haven't eaten for days."

Julie made wonderful lemonade, from scratch, ended all her summer appointments by serving it. In the winter she served tea. She went out and got the pitcher she kept in the refrigerator, sat us down with three glasses.

Meg said she hardly needed a massage at that point. That shaking had been an instantaneous massage. They decided to see how they both felt later.

"This brings up something I've been wanting to ask," Julie said to me. "I've been reluctant, knowing how you feel."

I nodded, took a long slug from my glass.

"How's your Spanish, first of all?"

"Julie." I shook my head. "My thing is zazen. Sitting zazen. I give people basic instruction."

"You're very good at that."

"I can provide a place to sit. Sit with whoever shows up. I deeply believe in all that. It's what I want to do.'"

"It's an admirable thing."

"It's all I know. And I don't really know that. I mean, what's to know? But it's the simplest and most profound thing I've ever done. To sit there."

"That's a wonderful task for your life. I completely support you. I want to do it with you."

"You two *are* getting back together," Meg said. "I can see it."

"We're not, sweetheart," Julie said. She turned to me. "I'm not trying to alter your goal for life. There's just this one other thing."

"Which somehow involves speaking Spanish? I speak street Spanish."

Julie heaved a sigh. "I have a housekeeper. Comes every other week to clean the place. I actually like cleaning but wanted to give this woman work, and she does a marvelous job. She's from Mexico."

"Illegal," Meg said.

"I'm sure. Her husband came four years ago to do construction, and she arrived a year ago. I haven't asked questions. But she has a twelve-year-old son who walks with a terrible limp. Painful to watch."

I could see it coming.

"Apparently she lived in some dinky border town and the boy broke his leg, a doctor set the bone wrong. I got my own doctor to take an x-ray. The medical answer is to break the bone and set it again, but she can't really afford that. She's also afraid someone will ask for her papers."

"I don't think that would happen."

"She's heard all kinds of stories."

It took just one person to make trouble.

"She has the idea I'm a healer," Julie said. "Doesn't get the concept of massage. There's a tradition of alternative medicine in Mexico, and a certain kind of person believes in that more. She thinks the right touch could heal her boy."

"So touch him. You have the same energy. I felt it when you massaged me."

"You have it more. I don't know why some people project it and others don't. Stone, for instance, is a wonderful technician, would give his proverbial left nut to have it but doesn't at all. His hands are dead."

"You don't know I have it more. You can't feel your own energy."

"You have it more than anyone I've ever met. I've had a lot of hands on my body."

No arguing with that.

"You have esoteric knowledge," I said. "That magic crystal that gives men a hard-on."

"You two *are getting back together*," Meg said. "It's so obvious."

"We're not, sweetie," Julie said. "He's making a joke."

"You do have the energy more, Hank," Meg said. "Julie's got it, but not like you."

"Maybe I don't want it," I said.

"It's a gift," Julie said. "The question is, are you going to pass it on?"

"You might have it for a reason," Meg said.

"There are no reasons," I said.

"You should use the gift if you have it, is the point," Julie said.

"What is it you want?"

"I want you to touch the boy. Vilma's going to bring him over, and I'll touch him a little, maybe use the crystal. That won't seem unusual. But then I thought you could touch him. Just the way you did me and Meg. No technique. Just touch him."

"And the point is?"

"To let Vilma see I'm trying. I also think you might heal him. I think it's possible."

"You healed me," Meg said.

"And me," Julie said. "Cancer seems tougher than a crooked bone."

The real reason to do it was that it wouldn't work. They would see that it hadn't and would get the whole thing off their minds. I could go back to sitting.

"If I do this once," I said, "and it doesn't pan out, I want you not to mention it again."

"Right."

"Don't be coming to me every week with some poor soul."

"Unless I get another headache," Meg said.

"Or my cancer comes back," Julie said.

Somehow this was never going to end.

*

"Hey, dude," Juan said when he and his mother walked through Julie's door. "Whazzup?"

He raised his hand and we banged fists, like basketball players. I'd never done that before.

"I thought I was going to have to speak Spanish," I said.

"*Not with me,*" he said in Spanish. "*With my little mama.*"

"Hi," Vilma said, giving me that limp handshake Mexican people prefer. "I'm very glad meeting you."

"We've been here a year," Juan said, "and she hasn't learned a damn thing, I swear. My papa's worse. He *won't* learn it."

Juan and Vilma were dead ringers, both chunky, seriously overweight. He—at the advanced age of twelve—was slightly taller, but only about five feet. He wore jeans and a mammoth t-shirt, had his hair cut short, wore a bright winning smile, constantly. He got the joke even if we didn't.

He did walk with a limp. Didn't seem to care.

"You're going to fix me up so I can play ball with my homies," Juan said. "Take on the honkies."

"Theese word," Vilma said. "No."

"Black guys use it," Juan said. "Why can't I? And the honkies call me all kinds of stuff. Wetback, spic, greaser." He said all this with that big grin. "How can you call me greaser with this head?"

He ran his hand over his bristly hair.

"We'll do what we can," Julie said.

"You got a nice place here," Juan said. "You two married?"

"Just friends," I said. "This isn't mine."

"He's my teacher," Julie said. "My Zen teacher."

"And there's nothing going on?" Juan said. "I bet." He punched my arm.

The kid was irrepressible.

"Where'd you learn this stuff?" Juan said. "Healing people."

"I studied at various schools," Julie said. "Hank just touches."

"You got the powah," Juan said. "I heard of that."

"Shall we get started?" Julie said. To Vilma, in Spanish: "*Shall we begin?*"

Before Juan said something even more inappropriate.

Vilma carried a ceramic image of the Virgin Mary, brightly colored, about eighteen inches high. It was—I would understand later—the Virgin of Guadalupe.

It was a Thursday morning, just two days after my talk with Julie and Dana. We'd asked Vilma to meet us at 7:30 so as not to interfere with her work, also so we would just have sat. I thought my energy was greater at that point.

I'd expected a pair of shy quiet Mexicans, hadn't realized Juan was such a stand-up guy. I saw that at the high school, children picked up English immediately, as if through their pores. Parents still couldn't speak after years.

"You can lie down," Julie said as we stepped into the massage room. "I'll light some incense."

"I don't have to take nothing off?" Juan said. "That's a break."

"I don't think so," Julie said. "Do you?" She looked at me.

I shrugged. How the hell would I know?

There was no telling what Juan might say if we had him strip down.

For someone who had never done this, Julie acted like an old pro (or a true charlatan). She lit the incense on the table at the foot of the massage table, put the image of the Virgin in front of it. She turned on some vaguely New Age music. She'd moved away from the Chinese stuff.

"This is just to relax you, sweetie," Julie said. "You want to relax."

"You don't have any of those ranchero tunes?" Juan said.

"Your mother believes in this. I'm picking up a little skepticism on your side."

"I'm down with it, really. I have a friend in Mexico who was brought back from the dead. His mama prayed to the Virgin. But we already tried that. The woman don't like me."

"She loves you," Julie said.

"*You need faith.*" Vilma lapsed into Spanish. "*You must have faith.*"

"We work with the power of touch," Julie said. "Energy moving through bodies. I've studied it and spent my life working with it. Hank just has a gift. I don't expect anything to happen this morning."

"I got a game this afternoon. I was hoping to dunk."

"But over time, I honestly believe this will help. I'm just going to touch your leg. Let me know if it hurts."

"I'm not some little kid. It don't hurt to the touch."

"Let's be quiet now, and hear the music, and feel your energy. It might help to close your eyes."

Julie stood there touching his leg. She had closed her eyes. Vilma took out a rosary and began to pray. The New Age music featured a flute above some quiet rhythm instruments. This was about as hokey a scene as I'd seen in years. All we needed was some Hare Krishnas dancing around.

After a while Julie picked up the crystal at the end of a string. She held it above his leg.

"This has healing properties," she said.

She didn't want to swing that thing too far. Get the boy all excited.

After a while she looked at me, stepped aside, and said, "Now Hank is going to touch you."

Juan was lying with his eyes closed. He almost looked asleep.

I touched him and his leg jolted.

"Whoa," Juan said. "Dude."

"Just let him touch," Julie said. "Let the energy go through."

"It was startling," Juan said.

"Try to hold still and let it happen," Julie said.

"It burns, like."

"That's the feeling of healing."

"It's running up my whole leg."

"Let's be quiet now. Let the healing work."

He lay there, though I could feel his leg shaking. I kept touching until, gradually, it got still.

By the time we helped Juan up from the table his mother had tears in her eyes. "*I felt the power,*" she said. "*Much.*"

Julie was helping him. "Does it feel different?" she said.

"Not now. It did, up there on the table."

He took a step and almost keeled over. "Whoa, dude."

"*I felt the power,*" his mother said.

"It's sometimes like this when I've been lying down," Juan said. "It'll come back."

I breathed a sigh of relief. If he'd stepped off the table without a limp I'd have been spooked.

He banged fists with me again. "Later, dude."

Vilma had to get to a job. She and Juan walked out to her car together. He limped badly the whole way. If anything, he looked a little worse.

"So much for that," I said.

"I'm glad we did it," Julie said. "Healing isn't always curing."

I didn't say as much at the time, but that was the last time I intended to go through that.

✻

Things got back to normal at the zendo. Meg started coming again on a regular basis. I had sworn her to secrecy about touching her. It isn't all that unusual to relieve a headache by little touching. By mid-June we had eight people coming virtually every day, Julie was the regular doan, Meg was being trained. I had the sangha I'd been hoping for all year.

On the following Friday Julie showed up early, before the sitting began, Vilma in tow. I hoped I wasn't teaching her zazen.

She carried her image of the Virgin.

"Juan is walking without a limp," Julie said. "Not even a trace. I didn't want to tell you until I saw him."

Vilma beamed. "*It was a miracle.*"

"I took him to my doctor and he took another x-ray," Julie said. "The bone has healed straight. He's never seen anything like it."

"*Thanks to God, and to the Virgin. And to you.*"

In that order, I hoped.

"You bean so good to us," Vilma said. "I wan you have this."

"I can't," I said. "That's yours."

"*I have another.* It weel help you."

"Help me?"

"When you touching others," Vilma said.

PART
TWO

EIGHT

"Dad." The voice at the other end was the most familiar one in the world to me, but I never heard it enough. "What the hell's going on down there?"

"How did you hear?"

"A friend sent me the news clip from YouTube. I watched it five times. 'That's my father up there,' I kept saying."

"I'm afraid so."

"The Oral Roberts of his generation."

"Expect a miracle."

The news clip started off dramatically, with a shot of boys playing soccer on the field behind E. K. Powe School, and a voiceover. "Juan Pedro Gonzalez wanted to play soccer with his friends, the young Latino boys he likes to call his homies, but he couldn't because he was badly disabled"—a major exaggeration, in my opinion—"the victim of a botched surgery when he was younger."

Shot of Vilma. "My boy wass lame. He very lame."

"Crip, they called me." Juan was talking with that huge grin on his face, the boys playing behind him. "Peg leg. Maybe some other names I can't mention on television. That's what they called me, these—other guys—at school." He didn't use the unfortunate word, thank God. "Now I can run like anybody." He ran back to join the other guys playing soccer.

Maybe not like anybody. Like a twelve-year-old kid who's badly overweight and hasn't run much for quite a while. But he could run. Kind of.

"What changed his condition was what his mother doesn't hesitate to call a miracle, though she doesn't know that word in English."

Shot of Vilma. "*A miracle. A sacred miracle. Thanks to God, the virgin, and the señor.*"

"The señor in question is a local high school teacher and Zen instructor named Henry Wilder."

"So," Josh said. "That crowd of people is lined up outside your place?"

"Julie Walter's. Remember her?"

"One of your girlfriends?"

"Kind of."

"They all blur together. That wasn't the clearest moment of my life."

Josh was thirteen when his mother and I split up, and he was quite angry for a while. It didn't help that I was out of control.

"Very tall," I said. "A pale complexion, slightly pockmarked. Tan glasses, big frames."

"Oh, right. And those huge boobs."

I should have mentioned them first.

"They were totally mesmerizing to a thirteen-year-old," Josh said. "The woman never heard of a bra."

"Indeed."

"She was nice. I do remember."

"She's given me the use of her house. She does bodywork, has a separate room for it."

"She was in the news clip too. The woman you cured of breast cancer."

"Supposedly."

"That must have been a pleasure."

"Josh."

"No, seriously. I'm sorry. It's not a joke. I know. But she didn't look the same. You guys are getting old."

"You're not exactly thirteen anymore."

"So how did this happen? I thought you were a Zen teacher."

I told him the whole story, with Julie, Dana, Juan. Of all the people in the world, he was the one I could most spill the beans with, be entirely myself. I should have called him long before. I never wanted to bother him.

"Now I'm in a mess," I said. "The whole Latino community shows up at my door, or at Julie's, every day. Women bring their children. Young men, their mothers. Grandmothers. They're not just from Durham, from the whole Triangle, surrounding towns. Half the time I hardly know what I'm touching, what the problem is."

It had started soon after Juan got better. He may have spoken up, but Vilma was the real emissary. The first people who came were respectful to Julie, but they all wanted to see El Señor. She begged me to join her.

"They're all Latinos?"

"Mostly. A few New Age types. Hypochondriacs and incurables."

"And you cure them?"

"I have no idea. All I know is they keep coming. It's incredible the number of people who need healing in this world."

"Like, everybody."

"At a minimum."

"And you're there all day."

"Julie set a limit. We go over after breakfast, people already lined up—she comes with me to the zendo—and we call things off around one. It's a long morning."

"For sure."

"She's got to have time for her bodywork. And I've got to have time, period."

"These people pay you?"

"We won't let them. Sometimes they leave something anyway, so we use it for the zendo. Where business is booming, by the way."

"I don't doubt it."

"They bring food too. All kinds of stuff. Want some tamales?"

Josh laughed.

"So what do you make of it?" he said.

"I just think Mexicans believe in this stuff. Alternative healing. The healers themselves haven't made it up here from Mexico, by and large. And I'm not part of the system. Won't ask them for papers."

"But what do you make of what you've done? Julie, and that kid."

That was the harder question. And I was talking to my son.

If you think you're enlightened, people used to say, ask your wife. Your son will do as well.

"I have no idea. Ever since I started sitting, but especially ten or fifteen years in, it's all been about energy. Energy moving through my body, feeling myself as energy. I know it drives you nuts, hearing about this."

"That's when I was a kid."

"It's weird enough having a father who does this."

"I'm over that. I'm interested."

This was new.

"Anyway. I feel this energy, moving all around. Sometimes it moves into my hands. I wondered at times if that was healing energy, if it would help somebody who was dispirited or ill."

"So you thought you'd try it?"

"Never. But Julie had this recurrence of breast cancer. She seemed so sad when she told me, in so much pain. I wanted to do something."

"To cure her?"

"That never came to mind. I thought it might help. Touching helps."

There was another major pause on the line.

"Jake always used to do something, when somebody was in distress," I said. "He didn't ask why or how. Just did it."

"Never anything like this."

"No. But he's not here, so somebody has to step in. You don't know what to do. You just do something."

"He ran the zendo. Talked to people about sitting."

"That's still what I'm doing, as far as I'm concerned."

"Not to the Channel 11 News Team."

"They never get the real news."

They did, to their credit, mention the zendo, show the group sitting.

"Have you thought about stopping? Just refusing to do it?"

Only every day.

"There's something about these Latino people," I said. "Quite hard to describe. It's not me they're coming to. I'm just what this thing is coming through. There's a figure of the Virgin Mary behind me, and they cross themselves when they see it. Look up at that as they talk."

"Huh."

"I've never seen such innocent faith and devotion. I get something from these people. And they get something from me. This energy. I don't know why I have it."

"Do you teach them zazen?"

"I haven't wanted to make that a condition. Some of them come and sit with us. It's perfectly natural to them."

It's like prayer, they said. It didn't seem strange.

"Most of them have what they need. With the Virgin."

"Right."

"It's not like they believe some doctrine. It's much more primal. Like a faith in life."

"It's fascinating."

"I know."

"I'd like to film it."

"*Eyewitness News* did that."

"I'd do it right."

Josh had started off as a film critic, did quite well with that, worked his way up to a column with the Boston *Globe*. But he'd gotten to a stale point in his career, one of those moments when he needed to move on. Jake had advised him, right before he died. Go write a screenplay. Something.

His screenplay was about a thirty-something guy who had trouble committing to women. Not the most original idea ever, but he made it into a riotous comedy, and it spoke to people in his generation, men and women. Apparently this was a big problem to his age group. He did make passing reference— and give a brief cameo—to a father who had committed when he was young, then hadn't been much good at keeping the commitment. I told him I'd be glad to do the cameo, but he got some old Broadway duffer. It was just a few lines.

Josh directed as well. He didn't try to hide the personal con- nection; his character was named Josh, and the movie was *Just Joshing*. It was amazing that he got to do all that, but he was an operator, and there were rumors that people were afraid to say no to him because he might give them a bad review. He advanced quite rapidly.

It hadn't been a smash but had a substantial indie following. He hadn't come up with another project. He'd been struggling for months.

"I'd do it as a documentary," he said. "It could be deeply personal. I haven't thought of the ramifications. But there's something about this situation that's so interesting. You not really knowing what you have. Them having something you need. The way two groups have come together, two religions. Don't you think?"

If anyone else on the face of the earth had asked me my answer would have been instantaneous. The whole thing was already enough of a circus. But this was the one person I hated to turn down, and whose company I couldn't get enough of. He was the one person I felt completely free about talking with. Though not on camera.

"When would you come?" I said.

"I'd fly down tomorrow."

Irresistible.

*

It was an oddly monastic life I lived, quite fulfilling. I was up at 5:00 in the cool of the morning, what cool there is down here. I shaved and showered, did some yoga stretches, rode my bike up to Ninth Street, which was deserted at that hour. I unlocked the door to the zendo unless Julie had arrived first; we laid out mats and cushions, readied a simple altar, and I went into the little side room where I changed into my robes.

Meg carried the incense; we entered together. Julie kept time, or somebody she had trained did it. We had ten or twelve people most days, but there was a lot of turnover. People came for Saturday instruction, and some would start sitting, but by the time they joined, others had dropped out, so we never ran out of spaces. The core of regulars was eight.

Sitting shouldn't be different from anything else. The real Buddhist life is to pay attention to everything. But there is nevertheless something special, even about the posture—it's not the same to sit on the front porch in my rocking chair—and that first period of zazen is the most peaceful time in the day for me. My mind isn't necessarily quiet, or untroubled. But for forty minutes I let it all come and go, am just a human body sitting.

I don't know why everyone doesn't do that. Talk about healing: it's the most profoundly healing thing I know.

We sit for forty minutes, walk another ten, sit for thirty. Sometimes during that second period I go off to that small room and do the conference—dokusan—that the teacher has with his students. New students settling into their practice—and that was all I had—want that often. But I never miss that first forty minutes. It's the one dependable thing in my day.

We used to go to Whole Foods for breakfast, but after the newscast things got too hectic, what with people stopping at the table, so now we go to Dana's for granola, fruit, and tea, sit over our tea for a while. Anyone can come, and Dana makes great granola. No one was supposed to show up at Julie's before 8:30, but there was always a line of people by the time we got there.

The whole situation was weird, certainly nothing we'd set out to do. It came up, and we responded.

Julie interviewed people before they came in, told me what was up as best she could. Often those who came in launched into a whole new explanation once they saw me. I listened, didn't always understand, but listening is a part of healing. The feeling came through loud and clear.

We removed the massage table for these sessions; I sat on a mat and cushion more or less in zazen, though I didn't make a big deal of it. That was how I felt most in touch. For our visitors we had chairs for those who needed them, but the folks who came to us didn't find it strange to sit on the floor. Behind me was a small table with a couple of candles and the effigy of the Virgin. Everyone, but everyone, crossed themselves when they saw that; palpable relief came over their faces.

Faith was what I saw as they sat there. Pure faith. It wasn't that they demanded a cure, even expected one, though they were hopeful. But they expressed the wish, threw themselves at the mercy of Whoever was in charge.

"*Why is the Virgin working with you?*" was the most frequent question I was asked.

"*I don't know,*" I replied, shaking my head.

"*Don't know,*" they repeated, also shaking their heads, smiling. "*Who knows?*"

Nevertheless, their fears, hopes, and concerns poured out. Often someone would bring a member of the family, their child, mother, grandfather. That person might seem embarrassed or shy. Eventually there would be a moment when it was time to do something. "*Where is the pain?*" I would say. "*Where would you like me to touch?*"

The expression on the person's face was a mixture of pain, fear, and hope. Often they cried when they felt the touch, tears of sheer relief. Often the people with them cried. Sometimes I did. We went through boxes of Kleenex. People were holding my hands, shaking my hands, sobbing, as they left.

How can you do that? somebody would ask when they heard about it. It was the first question Josh asked, essentially. How can you sit there and pretend to listen, not really understanding, then lay your hands on these people with no idea what you're doing?

I can do it because I know that listening is the most profound thing we do for each other—really being present and listening. Jake taught me that—the best listener I ever met. The emotional transaction is the important part. I also believe that human touch itself is healing, quite apart from miracles, from somebody being cured of cancer or a botched surgery. I believe that everyone has within them the energy that heals; all a healer does is free it, allow it to flow. And I believe that these things are important, whether the person is cured or not. We should come together and touch each other. We don't know how healing that might be.

I hadn't put those feelings into words before I did all this. It was doing it that helped me put it into words.

I played down with Josh the fact of people paying, but everybody brought something. Some did bring food—the whole zendo ate Mexican for weeks—and others insisted on leaving money. Julie left out a basket because it seemed necessary—as far as she was concerned, people could leave money or take it. We put it into a separate account, didn't consider it ours. We did buy things for the zendo.

By 1:00 we had done all we could, though often people were still around. Julie gave them *billetos* that moved them to the front of the line the next day. No one ever objected. I walked back to get my bike—all of these places were in easy walking distance—had lunch and took a nap. I was exhausted. In the afternoon I took a swim at the Y and came home for a quiet dinner. I did the Rosetta Stone computer program to learn more Spanish; I studied the *Shobogenzo* of Eihei Dogen, an ongoing project; I sat one last period of zazen and went to bed.

Once a week Julie had me over for an evening of bodywork, which could last any amount of time. "You need to be touched yourself," she said. "If you don't have a sex life you at least need to be touched. I don't know why you don't get out more."

When would I get out? Anyway, there was something about the simplicity of that life that I deeply appreciated.

Julie insisted our relationship was not sexual, but sometimes toward the end of the massage she had a little lapse. I certainly wasn't going to object.

I didn't think we'd include that in Josh's movie.

NINE

"Success is a bitch, isn't it?" Josh said.

"You should know," I said. He was the most effortlessly successful person I knew.

"Failure isn't the greatest," Julie said.

"Maybe you should try it," I said to Josh.

"I may have to," he said.

He had shown up at Julie's as our day was coming to an end. "The yellow house on Iredell," I'd told him, "before you get to the car wash," and as it turned out, there were four yellow houses—I hadn't noticed—but he could tell by the cars out front which one was hers. I had seen one last little old man, who knew virtually no English and who crossed himself constantly, looking toward the Virgin. Julie had spoken to the three families who didn't get to see me, explaining that their tickets would move them to the front of the line the next day, whenever they arrived. We sometimes had trouble persuading people to exercise that privilege.

"But *el señor* is here," they said.

"*His hands are tired,*" Julie said. "*They've lost their power.*"

"*No more power,*" the people said. "*We'll come back tomorrow.*"

While she was explaining things, Josh showed up.

I still vaguely think of him as the gawky kid he had been as a late teenager, all arms and legs, flaming curly red hair that he wore long and all over the place. Even in that persona he did well with the girls, totally unselfconscious, but he'd filled out since then, wore his hair closely trimmed along with a neat narrow beard. He dressed carefully, in nice jeans and a polo shirt, light jacket; he always looked casual but well-put-together. He wore his success lightly, never threw his weight around. He slipped into Julie's as if he were one more little old man, looking for healing.

"Let's go out," he said. "I could use some lunch."

"You two go," Julie said. "You need to catch up."

"There's time for that," Josh said. "I want to talk to you too. Make sure this is all right."

Josh was a diplomat. She was the one he needed to persuade.

I'd started going to the little Mexican eateries that had sprung up since the immigrants arrived. Durham had always had Mexican restaurants, but lately there was another kind of place, simpler but more authentic, a clientele that was largely Latino, tables full of men eating soups and stews, beer bottles all over the place. The tacos were soft, tortillas made on the premises. They could also be filled with items—like brains and tongue—that you couldn't get before.

I'd started reading about Mexico, studying Spanish, even watched *telenovellas* on the local Spanish station, though I couldn't follow the rapid-fire dialogue. But the dramas were easy, emotions broad and obvious. It was high opera.

I took Julie and Josh to a taqueria in the neighborhood, one of a half dozen within a five-minute drive. This one had a larger menu than the others, also served beer, which seemed appropriate for Josh's homecoming. He ordered *carne asada*, a thin grilled steak; Julie had *pozole*, a thick soup full of hominy; I had *tacos al pastor*. Negra Modelos all around.

"I loved *Just Joshing*," Julie said. "You must have been thrilled when it did so well."

"There was a huge amount of luck involved," Josh said. "Things just fell into place."

"I never went through that agony about romantic commitment," Julie said. "But we all have fears of deciding."

"You've just done that with Zen," Josh said, "according to Dad."

"After a lifetime as a dilettante," she said. "When I have one foot in the grave."

"You look in perfect health to me," Josh said.

"Thanks to your dad."

Josh flinched, smiled too quickly. I could tell he didn't quite buy that.

He wasn't the only one.

"Everything I ever did has led me to this," Julie said. "Therapy, biogenergetics, yoga, tai chi. You do those things and have the feeling it shouldn't all be so complicated. Finally you give up and sit down, and the thing you're looking for emerges."

Julie was a mature human being, that was the truth of the matter. Those things she had done weren't wasted. By the time she got to zazen she didn't have much resistance.

Halfway through the meal we ordered second beers, in the grand Mexican tradition. Bring on the tequila.

"Your new project sounds exciting," Julie said.

She said that despite major trepidation.

"For months I've been waiting for the next thing. Staring at my computer screen in a funk. Really floundering, I'd have to say. Then all of a sudden I hear my father's on the news, and a YouTube of the broadcast gets umpteen thousand hits. The zendo's thriving. People are coming to your house so he'll touch them. The whole subject fell into my lap."

"That's the way it should be, right?"

"But my father's a faith healer, out of nowhere. It's a shock."

"Not to me," Julie said.

"I don't know that I believe it," Josh said. "I'd have to say I don't."

"I'm with you," I said.

"When it happens in your own body you have no doubts," Julie said.

"Anyway, the question of whether or not you believe in such a thing could make a whole movie. A good movie. There's also the sheer coincidence of all this. If you two hadn't met that day, none of it would have happened."

"That energy would have found people over time," Julie said.

Josh frowned but plowed ahead. "Then there's the whole Latino issue. Why they as a group flock to you. Has anyone else been healed, in the whole community?"

"I've wondered," I said.

"They believe in this, and know a healing presence," Julie said. "It's obvious they get something they need. It's not just about results."

People came with conditions I'd never seen, pains I'd never imagined. I opened to them, and energy was released. Even I could feel it. I was tired at the end of a day, bone weary, also tired from hearing all the stories. But the energy was strong. I was exhausted and full of energy all at once.

"Where does it end?" Josh said. "Do you give up your job? Or at the end of the summer do you say, I'm sorry, I know you're sick, but I've got to teach high school?"

"We haven't thought about that," Julie said.

I had.

"Where do you get money if you just quit?" Josh said.

"The money pours in," Julie said, "though we never ask. We don't know what to do with it."

"So you'll make a living that way? Is that even legal?"

These questions were not new to me.

"There's also the question of where this began, in your life. Did it all start that first day you took a meditation class, which I happened to be present for? And how do people who know you feel? The guys at the Y. Students at high school. My mother."

Good Lord.

"There's plenty to look at," Josh said. "But it starts in your house, Julie, if that's okay."

"My concern is that these people are illegal," Julie said. "They won't want to talk."

"There are ways to handle that. I won't blow anyone's cover."

"I don't want you to interfere with your father's work. It's not a sideshow."

"I know. But what's going on here is rich and complicated. Everybody has an opinion about it. That's my subject."

*

"That woman adores you," Josh said later, back at my house.

"I don't know."

"And she's fiercely protective. A lioness."

Josh had been driving us around in the SUV he'd rented. That in itself set Julie off—as a kneejerk environmentalist—but he had lots of equipment. He dropped her at her place and we retrieved my bike, drove to my place on the other side of Club.

I'd bought a little house in the same neighborhood we lived in when Josh was growing up, used the money from Jake's place in Bar Harbor. It was shady and quiet, the houses modest. I loved the old trees, towering over everything. I had my bedroom in front, a meditation room in the back, guestroom in the middle. I told Josh he was welcome, but he didn't want to feel like he was twelve years old again. It also wasn't kosher to stay with the man you were profiling, apparently. Even if he was your father.

We sat in the living room, sipping coffee.

"So what's going on?" he said. "Is she your girlfriend?"

"You're asking for the movie, or for you?"

"I am the movie, at this point. I won't put in things you don't want."

Famous last words.

"I go to her for bodywork once a week," I said. "Somehow it's important to what goes on. I take in stuff when I see those people and she helps me get rid of it. She's the real healer. But sometimes a little extra something happens at the end. Because of our past."

If there was the least bit of wanting on my part—at least it seemed this way to me—she didn't do it. But if the massage was somehow complete, my energy settled, she did.

Afterwards she gave me a little kiss and walked out. Never said a word about it, after that first time.

"I thought you weren't supposed to have sex with your students."

"It's not really sex."

"Thank you, President Clinton."

"And Julie doesn't seem like my student. I teach her and she teaches me. It's as if she already knows what I've got. Zen is the discipline. She knows what it's getting at."

I hadn't spelled that out before, even to myself.

"Besides. I don't decide. She does."

Josh laughed. "Seems like a fine distinction."

He stood, stretched, began to get his stuff together.

"I know there's a problem with undocumented people," he said. "At some point I'll want to do shots of Julie's, and we'll figure out a way. Right now I just want to talk to people. Won't bother you at all."

"Sounds good."

"I'm just going to sniff around for a while, see what develops."

An old friend of his from high school had a garage apartment that was free—though minimally furnished—and Josh thought he'd try that. He went off to have a look.

I took a snooze and headed for the Y, a little later than usual. I didn't normally have two beers at lunch. There was a mammoth black guy in the locker room when I changed to my suit. I hadn't seen him for a while.

"I saw you on TV, man," he said. "I go, 'Hey, I know that guy.'"

"Yeah."

"They bringing you tacos, enchiladas, all that Mexican shit. That's all right, man."

The broadcast made a big deal of the food people brought, which had been copious that day. I didn't remember enchiladas, but still.

"Maybe you can heal me these fifty pounds I got to lose. Lay you hands on that motherfucker."

"I don't think that'll do it."

"No shit."

"You've got to heal yourself."

"It's these pies and cakes, man. French fries. I'll come see you I get cancer or something. You do high blood?"

"Stay away from the fries."

"You got to cure me them fries, man."

The day builds tension in my shoulders, all through my

back sometimes, but a swim cures that. Yoga does too, but not better than swimming. I like to swim a long time, not be in a hurry. Water itself is healing.

On the way home I stopped at Julie's. A sign on the door said she was in session, so I sat on the porch. It was one of those blazing afternoons when you can feel moisture in the air, the clouds seem to be hovering at about fifteen feet, but the rainstorm just won't happen. It's agonizing.

After a while Julie came out with her client, who looked blissful. She gave Julie a long hug, even hugged me. Julie and I stepped inside.

"So," I said. "What do you think?"

"I don't want him to scare people away."

"He understands that. He's discreet."

"He wants to get this movie done. That can wreck a lot of good intentions."

"We won't let that happen."

"You indulge your son, I believe."

"You can keep an eye on me."

Julie seemed defensive, frowning and pale, but stood up for herself well. I didn't think there would be problems.

"He wants to know if you're my girlfriend," I said.

"For the movie?"

"Just to know."

"And?"

"I wasn't sure, to tell the truth. Things have happened so fast."

Julie frowned, staring at me. "Honestly, Hank."

"You'll have to forgive me. Men are a little slow."

"That's supposed to improve with age."

"Even deeply enlightened men. With extraordinary healing powers."

She reached out a finger to touch my nose.

"At least I know to ask," I said. "Know who has the wisdom."

She put her arms around me. "I'm way beyond your girl-friend." She kissed me.

"I figured. I just didn't know the term."

"There is no term."

"Shouldn't we invent one?"

"It's beyond words." She kissed me.

"Does that mean we're going to the massage room?" I said.

She shook her head. "The bedroom."

TEN

Josh called Julie the next morning—unprompted by me—to say he'd stay away from her place altogether for a while. He would talk to Juan—who obviously wasn't camera shy—and his mother, see if they could get him entrée into the community. He promised he wouldn't force himself on anyone.

"Did you know he's fluent in Spanish?" she said to me.

"I knew he took it. Didn't know he was fluent."

"He did lit and conversational. Speaks better than I do."

Josh had never told me about his academic career. Thought it was his own business.

He said he'd like to do some filming at the zendo, just to capture the atmosphere. He thought he'd just have to come one day, asked if Friday was all right. Julie could send out a notice and people could stay away if it bothered them.

He was shrewd to make Julie the gatekeeper.

Her email about the filming had the opposite effect, especially when word got out who was doing it. People came who hadn't been there in weeks. A normal weekday might get fifteen, but we had twenty-four that day. They did their best bows. The chanting was a roar.

At Julie's place that morning the first man who came in had congestion in his chest, a bad cough. I asked if he'd seen a doctor and he said yes, but he wanted to see me too. I wasn't sure I believed him. I told Julie—after I'd touched his chest—to give him the information. We'd found two urgent care places that assured us they weren't interested in documentation. We had lists of rates and addresses, phone numbers.

"*You need a doctor*," she told him. "*It's very important.*"

"*I understand.*"

Next came a young man with a severe cleft palate, accompanied by his grandmother. "*It's not possible*," I told her. "*I can't cure him.*"

"*It's his head*," she said. "*His head.*" The problem was there, she seemed to mean.

I touched him for a while. His face seemed to soften. He had looked terrified.

The next woman was a young mother with a developmentally disabled child. Severely so. This was looking like a bad day. Again, I told her I could do nothing. The child was created by God this way. I couldn't change that.

"*But touch him*," she said. "*Please touch him.*"

I did. I didn't see what harm it would do.

The next guy wasn't Hispanic. He had curly black hair, a dark mustache and beard. He was six-foot-four or so, massively built, relaxed. He crossed himself, like the others, when he saw the Virgin.

"Your cure rate hasn't been great today," he said. "The cleft palate. Developmentally disabled boy."

"The first guy had bronchitis or something. I'm zero for three."

"What's your usual average?"

"I might be zero for the whole time. I have no idea."

He broke into a big smile. "Do you know who I am?"

I knew where I'd seen him. Same place I saw half of my friends. "You work out downtown. Wear a weightlifting belt." I'd seen him do reps with 225 on the bench.

"I hadn't noticed you."

"But you saw me on TV."

"Not even that, I'm afraid. People told me."

"You look in great health. Stronger than me. If your problem is a pulled muscle, I suggest a heating pad."

It had been that kind of day.

"I'm a priest."

"I don't think I can cure that."

He laughed. His laughter just about knocked down a wall.

"Those are my people out there, many of them. They told me about you. *El santo*."

"Good grief."

"It's a compliment. They aren't fooled."

"I haven't tried to fool them. I'm no saint."

This was unnerving.

"I was afraid you were bilking them," he said. "But they said you wouldn't take money."

"They bring it anyway. We have a basket now. Use it for our zendo."

"There's a woman in my parish who had terrible headaches," he said. "Probably just stress. Came to see you two weeks ago and hasn't had one since. There was a child with night terrors, who couldn't sleep. You touched him and he slept three straight nights."

"It could be coincidence. Meeting a friendly gringo."

"I'm a friendly gringo."

"You're their priest. That might not count."

"The woman with the headaches told me she felt the Holy Spirit in your hands."

"Good Lord. Pardon the expression."

"I don't want to take up your time. Could you come to my place and talk this afternoon? We could have lunch."

"Your place?"

"The church. Immaculate Conception."

"Let me treat you. I can bring it." If we had the usual contributions.

"You know where it is?"

"I've driven by."

"Come to the sanctuary. I want to show you something."

*

I'd seen Immaculate Conception from the outside but had never gone in. The sanctuary was huge, bright and open, not like the dim, lugubrious places I'd seen in Pittsburgh, where I grew up. There was a simple crucifix hanging from the ceiling, very plain, like a Giacometti. It clearly represented Christ on the cross—though there was no cross—but He also seemed to open his arms, welcoming people. There wasn't much other ornamentation. The place was quite plain.

The priest came out of a door down at the right, and I walked to meet him. Rows of pews formed a section on that side, and on the other side as well, so pews faced the altar on three sides. There was an alcove behind the pews, in it a huge image of the Virgin, like the small one we had in Julie's house. The priest turned toward it as I arrived.

"I didn't get your name," I said.

"Robert," he said. "Padre Roberto. To the folks who come to you."

He had on robes, which he hadn't earlier.

"You know who this is?" he said.

"The Virgin," I said. "I hear it all the time."

"Of Guadalupe," he said. "It's a wonderful story. Do you know it?"

I did, but I let him tell me.

She appeared to an indigenous peasant named Juan Diego in the sixteenth century, not long after the Spanish conquered

Mexico. The dark-skinned woman appeared to him on a hillside, and he understood that she was the mother of God, somehow of his God as well as Jesus. She said she wanted him to meet with the bishop and have a church built there. It was hard for a peasant to get an audience with the man, but he did. Still, the bishop didn't believe Juan Diego had seen the Virgin. He asked for a sign.

She appeared again and told him to pick roses from the barren hillside where they had stood, even though it was December and no roses should have bloomed. He carried the flowers in his cloak, and when he spilled them out before the bishop, there was a perfect image of the woman imprinted on his cloak. It had been hung in the chapel that the church built, had been hanging in some chapel ever since.

"You can still see it," Padre Roberto said, "at the Basilica in Mexico City."

I pondered the story, not wanting to offend him.

"You figure the peasant was just a great primitive artist?" I said.

"Where'd he get the roses?"

"That part could be made up."

"If an illiterate Mexican peasant could create that image in 1523, using God knows what for paints and colors, maybe that's miracle enough. But the cloth isn't suitable for painting, and the image hasn't faded in six centuries. The colors are strong, the fabric intact."

It was the kind of thing I wanted to believe, but it gave me trouble.

"I can no more understand that than your healing powers," he said. "What do you make of them?"

"I'm not convinced by them either."

"Tears poured from my parishioner's eyes when she told me. She felt the Holy Spirit."

I had no idea which one she was. There had been so many *dolores de cabeza*. It was a common complaint.

"I don't know a thing about the Holy Spirit," I said. "Don't understand the concept. But from the time I started meditating—anyway, two or three years in—I felt this energy. Wild energy that I hardly knew what to do with. A lot of sitting has been learning how to deal with it.

"For years it would do crazy things. Flip my arms. Turn my head this way and that. I had long periods, right out of the blue, when sitting was pure ecstasy. There was another period, five years long, when the energy pushed me back on the cushion, made my head go back and forth, like shaking my head no. It was all I could do not to flop down."

Padre Roberto shook his head. "Amazing."

"I saw bodyworkers, chiropractors, cranial sacral workers. One woman could actually make it stop. I'd sit the day after seeing her and feel perfectly still. But there were side effects. Dizzy spells. Disorientation."

He nodded.

"Finally Jake, the man who taught me all this, the biggest influence on my life, and who by the way was also the most ordinary man I've ever met, total salt of the earth—"

"As I would expect."

"He said, 'Are you exhaling?' I just stared at him. 'Every time you sit down,' he said, 'before you do anything, forcibly exhale, get all the air out. Then every time you inhale, make sure you've exhaled. Extend it out if you have to. Don't take air in until you must.'"

"And?"

"I never had a problem again. I sit completely straight."

Watch it start again tomorrow, of course.

"But I still feel the energy. I'm full of energy. My body bursts with it."

"We *are* energy, is what they say. That's all there is."

As we spoke, Padre Roberto had walked us out a side door, into a little children's park. It was deadly hot out there, no children around at the moment. He sat us down on a bench under a tree.

"You won't be hot in those robes?" I said.

"I'm used to them," he said. "The cross I bear." He laughed that big laugh again. It was infectious.

I had brought tamales, fresh that day. We got tamales almost every day.

They were a treat. I'd picked up a couple of Cokes.

"In a certain way it's easier in our tradition," he said. "If someone suddenly showed up with healing powers, we'd know where they came from."

As good an explanation as any.

"You could make the same assumption," he said.

"But why me?"

"Why anybody? I'm glad it's somebody."

I would have expected a priest to tell me to stop, at least severely question me. When he said who he was, I figured the jig was up.

All I really wanted to do was lead a Zen group.

The man could put away some tamales. He started on a third before I finished my first.

"Too bad we don't have some beer," I said.

"I could get some."

We could have walked about a block and bought a quart of Colt 45. That would have looked good, the saint and the priest.

"Our community needs what you bring us," he said. "Especially now. And it's good you're a gringo."

He seemed to be slowing down on the fourth tamale.

"How important do you think the attitude is of the person you touch?" he said.

"I've wondered."

"They call it faith healing. Who has the faith?"

"It ain't me. Hate to say it."

I thought of the people I knew. Julie? Meg?

"Do you know the boy whose leg I healed?" I said.

"He's your biggest fan. Him and his mother. They're the reason this whole thing happened."

"Does he have faith?"

Of all the untutored, profane kids I ever met.

"I don't mean belief in a doctrine," Padre Roberto said. "But Juan came to you expecting it to work. Totally without guile."

I suppose.

"What about the woman you cured of breast cancer?" he said. "Is she a woman of faith?"

"She's believes in everything. She's polyreligious."

"That's what I mean. That openness."

Don't tell that to the nuns back in Pittsburgh. They'll whip out the yardstick.

"I really think it would help," he said, "not that you need any help, not that everything isn't going beautifully. But I think it would help if you came here some Sunday. To the service in Spanish."

Holy shit.

"I don't know, Father."

"Not as a Catholic. Just to stand in front of the Virgin. Sit with these people as they worship."

"You don't think that's dishonest?"

"How so?"

"I don't believe in all this."

"So what?"

"Father..."

"I'm sure you have all kinds of ideas about Catholics. Everybody does."

Just the general Pittsburgh view. Tuna casserole on Friday and Notre Dame football on Saturday. Nuns who could wield yardsticks like martial artists.

"There are people in this congregation who don't think I should talk to you," he said. "Much less ask you to come. They think your healing comes from Satan."

Wonderful. "So what about them?"

"They won't be at Spanish-speaking Mass. They don't think we should have Spanish-speaking Mass."

I could believe that.

"They don't think we should have that image of the Virgin," he said.

It did seem quite Latin.

"But my ministry is to these people. That's why they brought me from Texas, because I speak Spanish and know the culture." It didn't hurt that he could bench press three hundred pounds. "I don't think this group knows Catholic doctrine, most of them. What they worship is deeper than doctrine, the same way Juan Diego did. God as a force. As overwhelming power. Immense love. They don't pretend to understand it."

I was with them.

"But they're happy to kneel before it. They'd like to see you kneel too."

They didn't have to explain it to Josh.

ELEVEN

"I think it's a great idea," Julie said. "I'll go with you."

We were lying in bed, staring at the ceiling. This was the second straight night I'd wound up in Julie's bed. I'd called after my meeting with Padre Roberto, wanting to talk, and she said she had appointments right through until evening; I could come around 9:30. That was perilously close to bedtime for someone who has to be at the zendo at 6:00, with everything set up.

Julie solved that problem by taking me to bed first, talking afterwards. She had a way of kissing—her mouth falling open like a trap door—that was instantly seductive. The night breeze blew in one window of her large bedroom and out the other. A large ceiling fan rotated above us. I wouldn't have thought you could be comfortable in North Carolina without air conditioning in the summer, but this was downright pleasant.

It had been years since I'd been in a woman's bed with her. I could start to like this.

"I was raised Catholic, you know," she said.

"I did not."

"Still consider myself one, in some fundamental sense. If you can be Catholic and Taoist at the same time."

Sounded like a hell of a combination.

"Do you go to Mass?"

"I go around Easter, especially Good Friday, which is the most moving service of the year. Occasional other times."

"You don't seem like a Catholic."

"There is no 'like a Catholic.' We go from the Berrigan brothers to Al Capone."

My own introduction to Catholic theology came at the age of six, when a neighborhood girl—one I had a strong crush on—told me I was going to hell if I wasn't a Catholic. She was a pretty Italian girl, with dark black hair in bangs. She had always been perfectly cordial in the past.

The Catholic kids had gone to public kindergarten with us, then switched to the Catholic school for first grade. That came as a terrific shock. I lost a number of good friends.

But not as much of a shock—according to that little girl, Christine—as the real separation would be, after we died.

"Have you ever burnt your finger on a match?" Christine said. I had, and still remembered the intense pain. "Hell is like that pain, but it's hundreds of times worse, on your whole body."

Sounded kind of tough.

"Have you ever pricked your finger with a pin?" The nuns had a way of coming up with the very things every kid had done. "Hell is like that, but the pitchforks are huge, much bigger than pins, and they burn like fire, they go through your whole body, time after time. It's worse than any pain we've ever had on earth."

The nuns hadn't wasted any time with the indoctrination. This was early September.

"The worst thing about it is, it never ends. It goes on forever and ever, no matter how much you want it to stop, how sorry you are for what you've done, how much you want to be forgiven. You wish you could go back to your old life and start all over, be a Catholic and be a good Catholic, but you can't do that. You never get out. Ever."

I wanted to ask Christine if this meant she wouldn't be kissing me again the way she had the year before (in her backyard, on the other side of some bushes), but didn't think that was the moment to bring it up.

I told all that to Julie as we lay there.

"Parochial education," she said. "There's nothing like it in the world."

"I take it you don't believe that."

"Never did. I knew the Protestant boys weren't going to hell. They were so cute."

Christine had no such qualms, the sadistic little bitch.

"I once heard a Zen master speak," Julie said. "Way before I knew what Zen was, but I went to hear him, up in Boston. He said one thing I'll always remember, when somebody brought up some other religion. 'Religion made up of words.'" She imitated his high voice. "'The Bible, Koran. Made up of forms. Bowing, chanting, singing, prayer. Words and forms not important. Drop words and forms; all religions come together. Where that place they come together? You have to find that place.'"

"I told Padre Roberto I don't believe Catholic doctrine and he said so what, more or less. The people worship a mystery, and I can bow to the mystery."

"About half the congregation is Latino when I go on Good Friday, half the liturgy in English. It's translated in the bulletin, but nobody follows along. They're not there for the words."

Still, there was something fundamentally strange about all this. *I* was planning to go to *Mass*? How did I get myself into this?

Julie turned my way and put her hand on my chest, lying on her side, began to rub my belly, my favorite part of her bodywork. She rubbed lightly, but with the whole of her palm.

"Has your sex addiction started to kick in?" she said.

"My what?"

She kept rubbing, paused for a few moments.

"You were always attached to sex, more than other men. Maybe too much."

I heaved a deep sigh. You hate to have that one thing about you brought up.

"A woman can feel it," she said. "It's endearing in a way. You want a man to like it. But it's a little off at the same time. Out of balance."

I felt anger stir in my belly—old anger, at myself, no doubt—but her hand rubbed smoothly above it.

"I've been careful," she said. "Didn't want to draw that out. At the same time, that energy is precious. You don't want to neglect it."

"I don't neglect it."

She kept rubbing.

"It's just that what I was doing seemed more important than sex," I said. "I shouldn't waste my time."

"Maybe so. I don't like that word 'waste.'"

"I gave so much to it in the past, ultimately so frustrating. Like a sinkhole."

"Yes."

She rubbed with her fingertips, very lightly, not so much with her palm.

"There's a way people do it as if they're looking for something," she said, "that they desperately need to find. They'll die if they don't find it."

I knew that feeling.

"But they never do," she said.

"Right."

"Because the thing they're looking for is here." She put her hand flat on my heart. "It's not out there."

"I know."

She was distilling Zen into a few words. It was the same with any human endeavor that people gave themselves to too much.

"There's a way to do it from a place of fulfillment," she said. "Where you're not looking for anything outside. It's just energy."

"Yes."

"That's what you're doing now."

"You can flip over into the other thing."

"I know." She was rubbing again, a little harder. "That's why I want to be careful. At the same time, I'm grateful to you."

"I'm grateful to you."

We lay there being grateful. I could have spent the rest of my life having my belly rubbed.

"Do you ever think," I said, "that healing energy is connected to sexual energy, and that the reason I've had it is that I haven't been having sex, at least not with another person, and that if I start having sex I'll lose it?"

The thought had crossed my mind.

"I hope you're not forgetting the astounding blow jobs you've been getting at regular intervals," she said.

"I don't know that I've healed anyone since they started. Except Juan."

"Right. Juan."

"I might have been shooting blanks the rest of the time. We don't know."

"I see healing all the time."

Through her eyes of faith. I didn't know how accurate they were.

"I don't think the energies are connected," she said. "I think they're the same. There's one energy. You dissipate it by chasing happiness outside yourself. Zazen recycles it. But that energy is infinite, from an endless source."

Julie spoke with enormous authority when she got started. I don't know where it came from.

"It flows through some people like a waterfall," she said. "I feel it in you all the time. I feel it now."

It was funny to be the one person who couldn't feel it, at least not the way she did. But I trusted her.

*

I hadn't known how to dress for Mass, but Julie said go casual. Except for the occasional little kid who insisted on a blue suit with his slicked down black hair, and little girls in party dresses, that's what everybody did. The men wore their best and brightest shirts, reds and yellows and purples, their cleanest dark pants, best cowboy boots. They didn't scrimp on the hair pomade. They glistened under the lights.

There were two Spanish masses, at 1:00 and 5:00, but Padre Roberto suggested we come to the early one, which was better attended.

Julie said we could go to the later one the following week.

What had I gotten myself into?

At the back of the sanctuary was a sizable cistern, I don't know what to call it, of holy water. Mexicans had a deep belief in that, Julie told me, sometimes took the water home. I should dip my hand in, touch my forehead, cross myself.

"I'm not Catholic," I said.

"Drop words and forms," she said. "It's a sign of respect."

I thought dropping would have meant not doing them, but what the hell, I took a crack at it.

Julie marched down to the front pew, not the place I would have chosen. We might as well have sat on the altar. She liked to be up front.

She knelt on the little bench and crossed herself, prayed for a while. I just tried to pay attention. When it comes to religion, that's all I've got.

"Everybody's looking at us," I said.

There were two substantial sections on either side of the altar, and every person in them—it could have been some weird optical illusion—seemed to be staring straight at us, boldly and unabashedly.

"That's what you want, right? People to see you're here?"

"I don't think they need to look every minute of the whole Mass." So far no one had blinked.

"We're the only gringos. We look weird."

We stood out like the proverbial sore thumb. A big white one, on a brown hand.

I soon found I couldn't understand the Spanish at all. A voice came over the loudspeaker announcing the beginning of Mass—gibberish to me—and everyone stood together. We turned to say hello to the folks who surrounded us, everyone proffering those soft Mexican handshakes, looking down shyly. They didn't look happy to have me. They looked profoundly uncomfortable.

I couldn't even understand Padre Roberto. He looked impressive in his Sunday robes, barrel-chested if anyone ever was, the tallest person in the room by half a foot. His Spanish wasn't in the least bit halting, blew right by me. I couldn't detect an accent.

One thing I noticed was the attitude of the congregation. They continued to look in the direction of Julie and me—I wasn't being paranoid. They looked around the sanctuary in general, maybe the men more than the women, who at least pretended to listen. The children were with them in the pews, or sometimes wandered from the pews, though never far (simultaneously frightened and fascinated by the big bad gringo).

They weren't especially quiet, and parents didn't try to keep them quiet. Babies were crying, children groaning and talking, occasionally screaming. That reached a fever pitch during the homily. Padre Robert talked on bravely, and you could hear him—he had a mike—but he spoke above a cacophony of screaming infants and children. Fathers sat in the pews wearing surly expressions, their arms folded as they gazed around.

All that changed when we got to the Eucharist. The whole crowd seemed more focused at that point, even the men. The odd thing was that not many actually took it, not even half the congregation. They felt they had to go to confession first, Julie said. That didn't stop her from blithely taking it, despite all those blow jobs she hadn't confessed.

Mass was centered on that ritual, even when people didn't take it. All the rest was just words.

There was great faith in objects, to an extent I'd never seen. People brought icons—crosses and images of the Virgin— and arranged them to the side of the altar, as if the ceremony would bless them. A few brought bottles to take holy water. Julie thought it might be for someone at home.

They would bless the people with water from a Food Lion carton.

I asked myself if Buddhism had anything similar. In a way all the trappings of religion are the same: we rang bells in our service of bowing and chanting, and we too offered incense, made ritual gestures.

You could say we were doing what the Buddha did: the same exploration of body and mind, examining our experience minutely. You could also see our zazen as a ritual reenactment of what he did. We followed his actions exactly.

There was a story about Sawaki Kodo, the Japanese teacher of Jake's teacher Uchiyama. When Sawaki was young he was new to the monastery and made to do menial tasks, work in the kitchen and elsewhere, before he was allowed to join the group. That may have been a form of discrimination, because he was an orphan, raised by a man who had been a gangster and a pimp.

But one day the monks were away—perhaps on their begging rounds—and Sawaki went in to sit zazen. A servant woman—someone who cleaned up, wasn't otherwise involved—happened upon him and began to do floor prostrations, one after another. Something in that image—an actual human being in that posture—seemed sacred.

In a way there is something logical about zazen—you can speak rationally about how it works—and in another sense it's as mysterious as eating a piece of bread and believing it is the flesh of a man who lived 2,000 years ago. You never know what might happen anytime you sit. The results are totally unpredictable.

My own recent life was a case in point.

"Shall we look at the Virgin?" Julie said when the service was over.

"We should." Padre Roberto had made a point of that.

A number of people went to that image instead of heading straight to the back, some praying, some just standing there.

"Cross yourself, Hank," Julie said.

"Again?"

"It's never the wrong thing."

Like bowing in the zendo.

So, in the midst of the little man with the bristly mustache and the loud Hawaiian shirt, the old woman hanging onto her daughter as if she could barely stand, the married couples who stood there solemnly, the children who glanced at me furtively as they held their parents' hands, I crossed myself. And promptly started to cry.

Tears poured from my eyes. I felt a catch in my throat and started to sob, not loudly, but audibly. I stood there and sobbed, quite helplessly. Nothing like that had ever happened to me.

Julie smiled, put her arm around me. "I told you it was a good thing."

"I'm not sad," I said. "It's just a feeling of love."

"Of course."

She cried too. I put my arm around her.

The children noticed first, then the parents. They cleared a way for us. I didn't need to get closer, or more centered, but that's what they were allowing. They were making a way.

I felt the release of crying way down into my body, into my balls, was how I would have put it. Like the energy when I sat, which came up from that place, it passed through my whole body, but moved down, away from my chest.

No one seemed surprised. The children might have been embarrassed. The old woman crossed herself. The man with the mustache put his arm on my shoulder, nodded to comfort me.

We stood there until the sobbing stopped. I took out a handkerchief and wiped my eyes, my whole face. We made our way out.

"Do you think you're Catholic?" she said.

"I have no idea. About anything, anymore."

We walked into the foyer at the back, and a woman stepped up to me. "*Thank you, señor*," she said. "*Thank you for everything.*"

"*It's nothing,*" I said.

She thanked Julie as well.

"Did you recognize her?" Julie said.

"I don't think so."

Three other people had thanked us by the time we got to the door. Padre Roberto was surrounded by folks but made a point of excusing himself, stepping over and shaking my hand, giving me his imprimatur. "Thank you for coming," he said. "It means a lot."

As we made our way to the car, four more people stepped up and thanked us.

"I feel as if I may have seen them," Julie said. "But who knows?"

"Not me."

"I'm not even surprised by what happened," she said, when we finally pulled away. "The Virgin is powerful."

"Apparently."

"You've taken on so much. More than you know. She's helping you."

*

I met Padre Roberto for lunch again that week, at his office instead of outside because it was pouring rain. He had a large desk covered with papers but cleared a space for us, had paper napkins and plasticware.

"I'm not supposed to do this here," he said. "But you've been so generous with the food." He reached into a briefcase and took out two cans of Modelo Especial.

"You even drink Mexican beer."

"It's big down in Texas. Quite flavorful. Let's hope one of the other priests doesn't walk in." We toasted with the cans. "Salud."

The lunch that day was *gorditas*, small thick tortillas stuffed with cheese and other things. The woman who brought them told Julie how to heat them, was honored at the thought that the priest would eat them. They made a great lunch.

Padre Roberto limited himself to five. I had the usual two. While he got started, I told him about my experience at the church.

"It doesn't surprise me," he said. "Might have surprised you."

"Indeed."

"I've heard experiences of the Virgin that would make your hair stand on end. Voices. Visions. Miraculous cures."

"But I don't believe in all that. Or in her, that I know of."

"Often the person doesn't think he believes. That doesn't seem the point. You're a person of faith."

Never heard myself described that way. "I suppose."

"You don't sit zazen every day for twenty years without faith. Call it what you want."

That was true.

"This has all been a bit much," I said.

"Buddhism doesn't talk about love, from what I've read. But I don't think your acts of contemplation are much different. More rigorous if anything."

"Might be."

"The place they take you has to be the same. There's only one place to go."

That's what Julie said.

"You've been giving love to people, whether you knew it or not. It's coming back."

TWELVE

I had thought I would see Josh all the time, but for that first week or so hardly saw him at all. He did the filming at the zendo on that one Friday morning but after that made himself scarce. I was afraid Julie had scared him away (though he didn't scare easily). She even remarked on the fact.

"I'm supposed to be chasing him out of my house all the time. Where is he?"

We hadn't heard from him at all.

Julie, on the other hand, had a whole new place in my life. After that first night I stayed at her place, we spent four straight nights together, sex every night. Not wild, maybe—I was pushing sixty—but still. And for all the meditation freaks out there who wonder what effect sex has on consciousness, I'd have to say it was major. We retired early, 9:30 or 10:00. Things took a while, as they tend to at my age, but we slept soundly. I woke with a sharp mind, felt clear throughout my body. The sittings the next morning were clear and bright.

Not that such sittings are a goal. It's just something to notice, all you celibates out there.

"This used to freak you out," I said one evening. "Having somebody in your space all the time."

"That's completely gone. Maybe it's having all these Latinos around, using the bathroom, wandering into the bedroom." Little kids tended to wander, and she tried to stop it at first, then figured what the hell. "But I don't think so. I think it was something about being cured of cancer or practicing Zen. All that stuff flew out the window. Now my life feels wide open. Anyone can come in."

That fourth morning, Meg stopped in on her way to zazen to return a book, and I was in the living room in my underwear, doing yoga.

"I *knew* you two were getting back together again," she said. "Didn't I say so about twenty times? Why did you deny it?"

I was flustered, sitting there in my underpants. At least they were boxers.

"It wasn't true at the time. You saw something we didn't."

"It was so obvious. The chemistry."

"Pardon the underpants. It must be strange to see your teacher this way."

"I've been around, Hank. They're cute."

Her spiritual teacher wore cute underpants.

"Wait'll I tell everybody," she said. "I mean, I won't if you don't want." She blushed. "Shit. Who am I kidding? I've got to tell somebody."

"Tell whoever you want. I don't want to keep secrets."

That's where the trouble begins.

That morning at zazen, everybody wore big grins as they bowed, walking out. Word had spread so fast? We'd been in silence the whole time.

At Dana's, afterwards, people wore the same grins over their granola. Nobody talked at all.

Finally Dana said, "We promise not to ask how he is in bed."

"What about her?" I said.

"We know how she is in bed. Most of us."

"We knew it was coming," somebody said. "Just a matter of time."

That afternoon around 2:00, Josh finally showed up.

"Are you about to head for the Y?"

"I can wait. Where have you been?"

"Busy. I had no idea how much legwork is involved in this. How much work, period."

I could imagine.

"On the other hand, it's fascinating. A wonderful Latino community here. Lots of them fans of yours. Though there are a few skeptics. What did you do to Stone Rockwell?"

Good grief. "How did you find him?"

"Small world. Doesn't matter. It's good to have a naysayer or two. Makes the whole thing sound honest. Speaking of which, I hear you're finally shacked up with Julie."

Jesus Christ.

"It's all over town. I think it's good, Dad. You were both in denial. Anyway, let me show you this. We can use my laptop."

He sat on the couch, motioned for me to sit beside him. He set the laptop on the coffee table.

"What do you mean, all over town?" I said.

"I'm kidding. Meg called me. She's one of my contacts. Glad to hear you're wearing boxers, by the way."

This was getting ridiculous.

He pushed a button and a face popped up, an older man, late fifties or early sixties. He wore a thick mustache, straw hat, and smiled constantly, some gold in his front teeth. He was chewing gum.

"You remember this guy?" Josh said.

"Not really. Lots of guys look like this."

"What you have to remember is, everything I'm going to show you will be vastly cut. There will be subtitles, possibly a voiceover. You only show the original clip for verisimilitude. It will be nothing like this."

"*Your father is a saint*," the man said. "*A saint from God.*"

"My father is a saint," Josh said. "Good title for a film."

"Please, Josh."

"It would have its ironies, of course. But it would capture people's attention."

"I'm missing this. The guy talks so fast."

I caught a few things, as he gestured. "*Power in his hands. Very strong power.*"

"What I love about this guy," Josh said, "is that he seems so down to earth. A man of the soil. He works construction. I love the way he smiles the whole time and wears that hat. And speaks so emphatically. All the gestures."

The man would rotate his shoulders, raise his arms, pull an arm back, smiling the whole time. A couple of times he crossed himself. He did have a winning manner.

"Basically he's saying he had arthritis," Josh said. "So bad he thought he'd have to give up work. He came to you and now he moves freely, can use a sledgehammer, a saw. We got some film of him working. He thanks the Virgin for you every day."

"It's always something like that. *I* have arthritis, for God's sake. Probably as bad as his."

"Physician, heal thyself."

"A lot depends on your attitude. How you feel day to day. It's easy to convince yourself you're better. Talk to this guy a year from now."

"He felt power from your hands."

"Everybody says that. I'm not sure it means anything."

Josh called up another image. "How about her? Remember her?"

She was a tiny woman, but chubby, with huge hips. She had long hair, way down her back. Again, she spoke rapidly, in a voice so high it was grating.

"Can't say as I do."

"This little woman cleans houses. Don't know where she got that voice. It's like she's singing."

It did have a sing-song quality. Just a little off-key.

"She somehow injured her shoulder. Goes into great detail about it. Lifting something down from a shelf. Hurt so badly she couldn't raise her arm. She was out of work five days. Went back because she had to. Still couldn't raise her arm. It was incredibly painful."

What she really needed was exercise. Her muscle tone looked horrible.

"When you touched her, she felt a warmth spread through her shoulder, all down her arm, through her back. The next day her problem was gone, she could work just like before."

"Sooner or later it was going to get better. Probably she was favoring it, afraid it would hurt. Don't you see a pattern?"

"There may be a pattern. But I have eight of these, and I'm not finished. The sheer volume says something. You could show one in detail, give snatches from ten others. And the words people use. Tears in their eyes."

I heaved a big sigh. "I do think something's going on. I have no idea what."

"This is my best one. How about this woman?"

The face was of a classic Mexican beauty. Dark wavy hair, dark skin, a luscious mouth, eyes that were sad, but terribly alive. "My name is Esmeralda Flores Macias," she said.

"Her I remember," I said.

"I'm a professor at North Carolina State University."

"I don't remember her speaking English," I said.

"She didn't. Listen."

"I heard about your father on television," she said. "Also at my church in Raleigh. The gringo curandero in Durham. The man with the spirit in his hands."

She stared at the camera in almost a mesmerizing way. Of the three, she was by far the most convincing.

You could hear Josh talking to her in the background, couldn't hear what he was saying.

"Yes," she said. "I was diagnosed three months ago. Lung cancer."

My stomach fell. I remembered it was something bad.

"Yes," she said, again to Josh. "I was a smoker. Brought this on myself. Whatever made me smoke." She looked down. "Why don't I tell it my way? Then you can ask questions."

"She was the only person who wanted to do it that way," Josh said. "So composed."

She turned her gaze back at the camera, stared at it, as if looking into herself.

"She was also the only person who really looked into the camera," Josh said, "instead of constantly looking at me."

She paused to collect herself, began talking.

"I had this diagnosis of lung cancer. And I was dealing with it in the usual way. Surgery, radiation, chemo. Staving off the inevitable. I said to my doctor, early on, 'This is a death sentence. Please don't bullshit me.' He said, 'You never know what might happen. But from a medical standpoint, yes. I'd have to say it is.'

"Then I heard about this man in Durham. This curandero. This magic healer. And I wondered."

She looked down as if to collect herself again. She told her story slowly, with long pauses.

"I'm not an ignorant person," she said. "I'm a professor of language at the university." She looked away. "Not that these others are ignorant. I just mean, I'm not the person you'd expect to see at a curandero. In my own country I might not go. But here..." She shrugged.

"So I didn't dress as a professor, dressed much more simply, parked my car at Whole Foods and walked. Didn't want to show up in a Volvo. I determined to speak only Spanish. I wasn't going to let on who I was. Just a nameless person with an ailment."

Nothing she did could hide her beauty. She'd looked like a princess in rags.

"The first thing about it was just standing, then sitting, in line, waiting for this man to see me. It was very humbling. There was a man with a disfiguring skin condition. Another who had been badly burned. A child who was disabled. An old woman who could barely walk. It was obvious that no healer on the face of the earth could do anything for these people. Yet here they all were, waiting to see him. And here was I.

"There's a story in Buddhism." She looked down. "I've been studying Buddhism since I saw this man." She glanced in Josh's direction. "Your father." Then back to the camera. "About a woman whose child has died, and who goes to the Buddha to see if he can bring the boy to life. He says he can, if she can just bring back a mustard seed from a family who has not been touched by death. She goes in search of that seed.

"That's what this experience was like. You have this condition, like lung cancer at the age of forty-four, and think, why me? Why do I have to go through this? Then you go to a place like that and see the other people. This little disabled boy. The burned old man. Hear them talk, share food with them. It puts everything in perspective."

It was the same way I felt every day. Lucky to be alive, to be healthy. I couldn't turn them away.

"Then this man comes in who was so ordinary, just an ordinary man. I would have expected ... I don't know what. White robes, a long beard or something. But here is this gringo. Didn't even speak good Spanish. Horrible accent."

"I didn't think it was that bad," I said.

"She's being harsh, Dad. You're trying."

"We went to see him, one after another. First we spoke with this tall, terribly white, rather unattractive woman."

"We'll cut that," I said.

"Definitely," Josh said. "It's gone."

"She'd have been fine if she had just combed her hair," she said, 'used a little makeup, gotten rid of those ridiculous glasses."

Julie could use some new specs. I kept meaning to tell her.

"She heard the basic problem. Then we went in to him."

If it turned out that I healed this woman, I was the greatest healer since Jesus Christ. At least Oral Roberts.

"He didn't look like he was having a wonderful day. The burn victim, the disabled child, the man with the horrible skin condition, all ahead of me. When his assistant came in, leaned down and whispered in English—'Esmeralda. She has lung cancer'—his face just fell. It fell about ten feet. It looked like the worst news he'd heard in his life. Nothing like the response of a doctor, who's been trained.

"He just sat there. He sat absolutely still, taking in this dreadful news. He said, *Would you like to speak with me about your condition?*" and it turned out I did, I went on and on, about how I had smoked, and I knew that wasn't good and now it had caught up to me, but so early, my God, so much earlier than I thought it would. Everything seemed so hopeless. My life seemed hopeless. But as I said that, it didn't. For the first time since I'd been diagnosed, I didn't feel hopeless. I was chatting away, giving him one more story of an impossible situation. I'm not even sure he understood my Spanish. But it was such a relief, finally saying all that. Something released in me.

"And when he touched me, I'm embarrassed to admit, I started to cry. Tears poured down. And *he* cried. In this whole thing, chest x-ray, cat scan, radiation, chemo, no one had touched me, in a simple human way. Such a basic thing. It made me weep. It was wonderful. Such compassion, such sympathy. I can't describe it. One of the remarkable experiences of my life."

She had started to cry, talking about it, but not hard. She wiped away a tear.

"So I started reading about Buddhism. Practicing meditation, with a group in Raleigh. The ambition of my life, whatever life I have left, is to sit as still as your father, hearing bad news. I never saw a man so still."

Again you could hear Josh's voice in the background. She looked his way.

"No. There's been no change. I'm still going to die. But I regard myself as one of your father's great healing stories."

Again she looked over toward Josh's voice.

"That's right," she said. "It's a koan. A koan for your movie audience." She looked into the camera. "All you out there." She smiled.

Josh pushed a button and turned it off. "That's it."

"Great God," I said.

"That's the whole movie, right there. Between the man who says you cured his arthritis to this woman, who is by far the most articulate person I've talked to, and who by the grace of God speaks English, those are the two poles. There's the simple understanding of the man, which is wonderful in its way, then there's this much deeper thing, what we're really talking about. But you don't want to lose the other."

"The question remains, am I doing anything?"

"How can you say that after hearing her?"

"Anyone could do that. A human touch."

"But you did it. That's the point."

"Some of these people feel power. That time I cured Meg of her migraine. You'd have thought I hit her with an electric shock."

"Seven or eight Mexicans say the same thing."

"Then there's this woman, who's really got something. Lung cancer. She feels nothing. A sense of release."

"Which in its own way is more than anyone else. Listen, Dad. No one's more skeptical of this than me. Somebody tells you your father is Jesus Christ, or even the Reverend Fulton J. Sheen, and you have a little trouble. But I for one am convinced. You've found your calling, in your own way. This is what you should do with your life."

But what was it, was the question. What was I doing?

"The centerpiece of this movie is going to be my interview with you. The son and the father."

"Then you become a monk and move to the Himalayas," I said.

"We'll skip that. But we should get started. It's going to take a while."

"I'll be happy to." Though I had no idea what I was going to say. "Right now I'm headed for the Y."

"Another group I want to talk to."

"Not today. Please."

I'd had enough. I went down and did my hour or so in the pool. Used to be forty-five minutes, but everything takes longer these days. Talk to Julie about that.

Often something comes to me as I swim. Talk about energy. There's a subtle, sometimes not so subtle, shift in energy: I go in feeling one way, come out quite another. I actually sometimes *think* something new, though the thoughts that pass through my mind are mostly crap. Worse than sitting.

That afternoon I went to the Y after the odd experience of hearing people talk about all this. I suppose—stupidly—that I was looking for them to answer a question I'd asked myself, about whether I was doing any good. When I got out of the pool, the question was gone, I didn't need an answer, and I knew what I was doing with my work. I knew what I would say to Josh in the interview.

Talk about miracles.

I also didn't care if I had the interview or not. I felt no need to say it.

I drove back to Julie's. She was waiting for me.

"Padre Roberto called," she said. "He wants to talk to you."

THIRTEEN

"Curing is when you remove some temporary condition," Padre Roberto said. "Like when you made that woman's headache go away. Healing is deeper."

He had been funny when I spoke to him on the phone. He hadn't said don't bring gorditas, or that he didn't like variety. He just made it clear that if any tamales came my way, that was the meal he'd prefer. He promised to see to it that we had some cold beer with them.

He had brought a number of paper napkins, set up some mock placemats along with napkins. He even provided plasticware and paper plates. The man was getting serious.

The last items, out of his bottom desk drawer, were two Modelo Especiales.

I had begun by telling him about the clips Josh showed me.

"Healing is what you did with the woman who has cancer," he said. "Curing is what you did with the others."

"Curing is what people want."

"Sometimes they get more than they bargain for."

All of this sounded esoteric and abstract. Padre Roberto spoke as if it were—pardon the expression—gospel truth.

"Do you think there's such a thing as curing?"

"Definitely. I knew a woman in New Mexico who could take anybody's headache away by using her hands. She learned as a kid. Made a whole career out of it."

"She must have been popular."

"Made a fortune. Some headache sufferers will pay anything."

Meg would have given all she had the day she had that headache.

"Some of us just have access to that energy. I don't know that you cured those people for good. You might see them again."

He had finished a third tamale, was eyeing a fourth as he sipped his beer. We're all subject to temptation.

"What about Esmeralda?" I said.

"Healing comes from God. Pardon me for being Catholic. But that's what I'd say. That's much deeper."

What do I have to do with that? was the obvious question. I didn't want to ask.

"You're an agent of God, from my standpoint."

He could read my mind, apparently. But he couldn't resist that fourth tamale. He was all over it.

"I don't see how that's possible," I said.

"Everyone has a term for the most basic reality. Buddhists say 'emptiness,' right? Or Buddha Nature?"

"I don't think the Buddha talked about it."

"Which might be the highest wisdom. But he felt it, don't you think?"

How would I know?

"How could you sit all that time and not?" Padre Roberto said. "The creative force of the universe. He knew his followers would too, if he could get them to sit. He didn't have to describe it."

This was a novel view of the Buddha's teaching.

"You've felt it, haven't you?" he said.

"I've felt something."

"People have felt it in you. It doesn't matter what you think."

On that we could agree. Thinking was no help.

"Healing is a miracle," he said. "Very rare. Completely inexplicable. And it inspires awe. I haven't seen the clip, but it sounds like the encounter with Esmeralda was healing."

What amazed me about Catholics was their certainty. A truly informed Catholic like Padre Roberto was firmly grounded in reality. But if I'd levitated and started flying around the room, he'd have had an explanation.

"So how was Mass for you last week?" he said.

"I didn't understand a lot. *Mi espagnol.*"

"It's a specialized vocabulary."

"I didn't get the homily. Julie explained it afterwards."

"That's the least important part."

An interesting statement from the man who gave it.

"I don't know if you could tell, but that was the official Spanish Mass, before the large Sunday meal. More people attend."

"Seemed like a good turnout."

"The second mass is sparser, but no less important. I was hoping you'd try that too."

"We were planning on it."

"This Sunday?"

"I guess."

"Because there's someone who wants to speak about you."

"Oh." Shit. "Padre, I don't know."

"A lot of people last week knew who you were."

"I figured." They were sure as hell staring.

"Any gringo causes a sensation. Including Julie. She's so unusual to them. Tall and pale."

If he mentioned the glasses I was out of there.

"She stood out in that crowd of small dark people. It was funny."

Watch what you say, Padre. I happen to be fucking her.

"But word spread through the community. The five o'clock Mass felt left out."

What the hell do you want from me, man? Two Masses in one day? It would kill me.

"They wanted me to ask you to come. And they want to acknowledge you from the pulpit."

"This is done?"

"All the time. Special announcements at the end. Wedding anniversaries. Girls' fifteenth birthdays."

"Do you know what the guy is going to say?"

"I have an idea. I'd rather let him just say it."

This sounded profoundly uncomfortable. I was self-conscious enough as it was.

"It would mean a lot," Padre Roberto said. "More than I can say."

"It's fine." I didn't see any way out.

"I wish I'd thought to bring some dessert."

There was always another tamale.

*

The later Mass had a different feel. The group that performed music was smaller, had fewer instruments. The acolytes were younger, didn't seem to know what was up. I would have to say, though, that the crowd was larger.

Word had spread about the acknowledgement, and some people attended who normally came earlier. It was a major coup for the 5:00 crowd.

I fortunately didn't know that at the time.

Julie again insisted on sitting up front, though I told her how edgy I was.

"You might block somebody's view," I said. "These people are so little."

"I'll block their view wherever I am."

"There's always the last pew."

"Don't be ridiculous."

Once again, Mass passed over my head. I remembered a few of the things we sang, so I could fake my way through them. Sometimes, when everyone was reciting, I found myself making vague mumbling noises, which Julie found quite funny. I wanted to join in.

During the Eucharist, Julie said I could walk up with my arms crossed in front of me, hands on my shoulders, which signified I wasn't eligible but would appreciate a blessing. Six other people were distributing the Host, but I went straight to Padre Roberto. He made the sign of the cross on my forehead. I felt the energy all through my body. The magic of touch. He had it too.

At the end of the service, a man stood to make announcements. He didn't speak into the mike, mumbled everything. I didn't catch a word.

"Did he say something about me?" I said to Julie.

"Not that I heard."

Another man stood up.

He was quite young—looked barely twenty—and strikingly handsome. I find Latinos in general attractive, but this guy was movie star quality. He also wore a suit, quite rare at Mass. He seemed nervous and slightly hurried, but paused when he got to the podium, settled himself. And—it seemed so simple—he spoke into the mike. His voice was clear.

Every now and then someone will speak Spanish who I can understand. I don't know whether it's the vocabulary or the way they enunciate. This man was like that. I didn't get every word, but I got the gist. I checked with Julie later and she confirmed that.

He said he had been married for four years, living in this

country for three. I hoped he was older than he looked. He came from the state of Guerrero but was living here now. He felt blessed to have found this church, and the wonderful people who worshiped here.

He said that when his wife was young, a doctor had examined her and said she could never have children. The man was sorry, but there was nothing he could do. Even before they were married—he blushed as he said these words; added, "*Pardon me, Padre*"—they had gone out for a year, and she didn't get pregnant that whole time. A number of people told him not to marry her, because he wanted a family.

"*But we knew that if God could give a baby to the Virgin*"—he gestured to the image at his left—"*He could give one to us.*"

The congregation beamed. Nothing pleased them like a reference to the Virgin.

In this country also, they had not been able to conceive, though they tried very hard.

"*You would understand how hard I tried if you could see the beauty of my wife,*" he said.

The man was a charmer.

They saw a doctor in this country, and he too said she would not be able to conceive. He was sorry.

"*But what did he know?*" he said. "*He didn't know the Virgin.*"

This guy might want to consider a television ministry.

Early in the summer, he had heard on television about a man in Durham who was healing people with his hands. He had never been to such a person, even in his own country. He wasn't sure he should do something like that, especially here. As much as he and his wife wanted a child, he felt unsure.

Then a friend of his, a woman sitting right here—he gestured to his right—told him the man had an image of the Virgin where he worked. "*I knew it would be all right.*"

"Do you remember this?" Julie said.

"Not yet."

At that point, I was about the color of the scarlet vestments.

"We went together to see this man. He did have an image of the Virgin. We told him our problem. He touched my wife's stomach. He held his hands there a long time."

"I do remember," I said. "I remember the wife."

I could see her sitting to the man's right, with the woman friend.

"It was a while back," I said. "When we first got started."

"My wife felt something move inside her. She knew something had changed. And that night. Of course I can't be absolutely sure. But I believe that on that night we conceived a child. In any case, some days later, the test from the drugstore came back positive. We went to the doctor who told my wife she couldn't conceive, and he agreed that she was pregnant. He didn't know how he had made such a mistake. He couldn't explain it."

"This is rather hard to believe," I said.

"Not for these people," Julie said. "Look at them."

The congregation sat in rapt attention.

"The doctor couldn't explain because he didn't know the Virgin. But we do."

The young man paused for a while. He couldn't have given this talk more effectively.

I was about as uncomfortable as I'd ever been in my life.

"I didn't want to come to this country," he said. *"Like many of you, I came because I had to, for my family. Many things about it have been hard. But now I'm happy I came. If I'd stayed in my own country, I might never have had a child."*

He paused again, looked out at the audience.

"I don't know why the Virgin works with this man. It seems strange, especially with him living here. But I don't know why the Virgin does many things. I don't know why she came to Juan Diego in the first place, except that she loves us. But I'm glad I found

Enrique Wilder. Henry Wilder. And I'm glad he could be with us today, so I could thank him with all of you."

He came from the podium to our pew. I stood as he arrived.

"Gracias, señor," he said. "Thank you very much."

"Thanks to you," I said. *"But it was the Virgin. As you know."*

His wife came to greet us as well. Didn't look pregnant to me, but it was still early.

"Gracias," she said.

"Thanks to you," I said.

Maybe I was in a state of shock. It was that kind of situation where the thing is happening but you're not quite in it, in this case because I was so embarrassed. If the Virgin Mary could have reached down and beamed me up at that moment, that would have been my miracle. She didn't do it.

There was supposed to be some official end to Mass. I didn't remember from the week before. But the thing I wanted was to get out of that sanctuary as soon as possible. I didn't want every person with a hangnail to come up and ask for help.

Fortunately, the way we had all stood—the man and his wife, Julie and I—led to our walking out. People looked around and craned to see us, but nobody left.

"I don't know the words," I said when I got out. My most frequent statement in Spanish.

"Hey, man," he said. "I speak English. I was just speaking Spanish in there."

"I'm so happy for you. What a story."

"We're grateful to you. We can never say."

"I think I should leave."

"There are many people who would like to meet you."

"That might be awkward. I'll come back. But I'd rather go now."

Padre Roberto was saying a few final words to the congregation.

"It's all right," the young man said. "I understand. God bless."

Julie and I made it to the car before the onslaught.

"We could have stayed," she said.

"I was so embarrassed. I'd have forgotten every word of Spanish I know."

"What a story. I was stunned."

"Do you believe it?"

"Of course I believe it. The doctor says the girl is pregnant."

I didn't see how it was possible. This was the greatest conundrum of my life.

FOURTEEN

The fallout from that incident was enormous. Unbeknownst to me, a reporter from the local Latino paper had covered it. He took photos during Luis's talk—which I didn't notice—and when the two of us shook hands. I must have really been out of it.

It was one of those moments when the two cultures reached out. No story sells better among Latinos than one about a child being born, especially one that involves the Virgin. In the midst of one piece of bad news after another, the paper was dying for such a story.

From the paper the Latino television station picked it up, then the city papers, then local television and radio. People interviewed Luis, who was as articulate in English as in Spanish. They interviewed Julie and me. Scenes showed up on YouTube. The local public radio station did an extended segment, including a long interview with me. I couldn't believe the territory it strayed into. The man began with the most basic question.

"Mr. Wilder, how much credit do you take for the miraculous pregnancy in the Latin community?"

He made it sound like a virgin birth.

"None whatsoever," I said.

"The father credits you. Father and mother both."

"That's very generous, but I credit their faith in God, and the miraculous power of the Virgin of Guadalupe."

"You believe in her power?"

"I have to. There are many incidents that show it."

"Is it normal for a Buddhist to believe in the Virgin Mary?"

"There is no normative Buddhist, as far as I know. Certainly not me."

"If you did have anything to do with the pregnancy, if you have some kind of healing power, what would you say?"

"I'm as astonished as everyone else."

"But many people, especially Hispanic people, credit you with unusual spiritual power. Where does that come from?"

"My spiritual practice is to sit and stare at a wall."

"That doesn't give us much to go on."

"It's an ancient practice. Been going on for thousands of years in the East."

"Yet you're associated with Hispanics."

"That's coincidence. The first person who came to me was Mexican. They have a tradition of alternative healing."

"It's controversial, but does it concern you whether people who come to you are legal?"

"It doesn't. Any more than it concerns you whether the people who bus your table at the restaurant are legal."

"Do you know if the couple who you helped are legal?"

"I don't."

It will come as no surprise that these two questions—entirely irrelevant to the real issue—got more attention than any others. We got more emails, more phone calls. Eventually Julie and I canceled our phone service.

"Finally, Mr. Wilder, a piece of human interest. The first person you 'healed'"—you could hear the quotation marks as he said the word—"purportedly of breast cancer, is the person who works with you. She has no connection, as far as I know, with the Virgin Mary."

"She was raised Catholic. She explained the whole tradition to me."

"And now she helps at the clinic."

"The clinic was her idea. She's also an important part of our Zen center."

"There are rumors that link the two of you romantically."

"Listen, fat boy, if you had any idea how that woman can suck cock."

Actually, I didn't say that. What I said was:

"The rumors are true."

"Some people question, in a religious community, whether it's appropriate for the teacher to be involved with his students."

"Normally it isn't. But Julie and I were involved before. We've been friends for years. We got close again in recent weeks and the romance just happened."

That was what we got the second greatest number of phone calls and e-mails about. Sexual abuse, dysfunctional families, the teacher overstepping his bounds.

The only person I've ever sexually abused is myself. However, I've forgiven myself.

Everything changed after that. The number of people who came to Julie's increased dramatically, including a number of non-Latinos. The number at the zendo increased too, to the point where we rented a larger space and bought more cushions. Some Latinos came to the zendo. Julie had to give instructions in Spanish. They asked Padre Roberto if it was all right and he said of course. Lots of Catholics practiced Zen.

The other—more subtle—change was in the kind of person who showed up. That was strictly a gringo phenomenon.

Often these new people had a spiritual bent, wanted to know exactly what our lineage was, as if minor matters made a huge difference. They had meditated "for years," they said, but that turned out to mean every now and then over a number of years.

They were deeply disappointed to find that all we did was sit there, figured there had to be something more.

And if they came to the clinic, they were vague about their ailments. Their symptoms were hard to describe, would come and go. They weren't necessarily active when the person saw me. Depression was often part of the picture.

The real problem was a low-level dissatisfaction with life. They hadn't found work they liked. Often they weren't working, had money, or were on disability. They'd never settled down with one partner or figured out their sexuality.

Julie was familiar with such folks from bodywork. It wasn't that their ailments didn't exist. It was that a certain kind of person turned up with them. And nothing ever cured them.

The person who most exemplified this new attitude was a woman I thought of as Whiny Wendy, which was unkind of me and also unfortunate, since there were a couple of times I almost said it to her face, as in, "Well, Whine ... I mean Wendy." She was extremely intense, rather thin, deeply worried, and showed up at Julie's in mid-July, not long after the interview on public radio.

Even as she entered the door—though she'd waited in line a couple of hours—she seemed not to know whether to come in or go back out. She wanted to get up as she sat down.

"All these poor people in their distress," she said. "It's so humbling."

The man in front of her was a Latino who had smashed his arm in an accident. I hadn't been much help with that. He also wanted me to bless a religious amulet.

"For me too," I said. "It's a reminder every day."

She had a great deal of trouble looking me in the eye, could only do it now and then.

"How can I help you?" I said.

"I have problems with depression," she said. "Suffered from it all my life. This overwhelming malaise, to the point where I can hardly get out of bed. I've talked to doctors about chronic fatigue, Lyme disease. Even HIV. I made some unfortunate choices early in life. But nothing's been diagnosed."

"You have physical symptoms?"

"All kinds. Stiff neck. Bad back. Quite disabling at times. I've been diagnosed with irritable bowel, also possibly Crohn's. I'm not feeling symptoms right now. That's often true. I make an appointment, then don't feel the pain anymore. Yet I spent the weekend suffering horribly. You know what I mean?"

"I do."

I didn't.

"It's gotten to the point where I don't know who to see. Which doctor to call. Sometimes I think it's a spiritual problem."

"I deal with those at the zendo."

"I know. I'm a friend of Meg and Dana's. But I didn't want to come there because they said you wouldn't touch them physically. I didn't want to burn my bridges."

"I didn't think touch was what they needed. I finally touched Meg for her migraine."

"And hugged Dana. I long for one of those ecstatic hugs."

"I'd be happy to hug you. I don't think it'll be ecstatic."

Especially because she hoped it would be.

I leaned across and hugged her, rubbed her back. If anyone ever needed a hug, it was her.

"The thing is," I said. "Everything you've told me this morning. Everything you say about your history. What I see as you sit here, is someone who doesn't seem comfortable. In her body, in this room, in the world."

"I see. That's interesting." She looked as if I'd explained an abstruse question of quantum physics. She held that for just a moment. Then her face collapsed. She bit her lip, convulsed into tears. "It's so true. I have never for one moment felt comfortable in this ... I don't know what I even mean. I don't feel I belong." She sobbed deeply. "That I deserve to be here. Not that I asked to be. What am I even doing here?"

"Deserve?"

"I've never found anything to justify my existence. The one thing that would give me a home."

I felt a discussion of work coming on.

"The thing I think most about Zen practice," I said, "one of the things it is most profoundly, is a way of feeling at home. In your body. In the world. I don't know how that happens. But it keeps getting deeper."

At home in the world was a feeling I often got from sitting.

"That's the message of every religious tradition. You have every right to be here. Don't need to justify yourself."

"I wish I could believe that."

"You don't need to believe it. You need to know it in your bones."

"It must take a long time."

"It does and doesn't. Begins the first time you do it. Goes on forever, getting deeper."

"I don't think I can sit too long at a time. Meg told me forty minutes."

"There's a thirty-minute sitting too."

"I probably can't manage five."

"You do your best. Move if you have to. Start with five at home, work your way up."

"It would take forever."

"You've got forever, according to Buddhism. Have you got something better to do?"

I didn't think zazen was the answer for everybody. Actually, I did. I didn't suggest it for everybody. But Wendy seemed a prime candidate.

"This means you won't touch me?"

"I'll touch you anytime. I'll make an exception. Where would you like me to touch today?"

"My stomach, the way you did for that woman on TV. So many of my problems are there."

I touched for a while. She continued crying. Her body shook. There was a lot going on.

She did come to the zendo, as it turned out. She was sporadic, but she came for the rest of the summer. And she came to Julie's often, at least once a week. I touched different places. There was always a lot of vibrating, a deep emotional response.

"You don't have to come here," I said one day. "I could do this at the zendo."

"I like coming here. Being with these people. It's part of the healing."

I felt the same way. I was never sure what was being healed.

The next person who came on Wendy's first day—the gringos clustered together—couldn't have been more of a contrast.

He was small, slight, and dark. His hair was cut short, he reeked of cigarettes, and his arms were covered with tattoos. He had a nose ring between his nostrils. That always looked horribly painful to me. He had another on his left eyebrow. Ditto. He seemed terribly nervous, terminally shy.

"I take it I can't smoke in here," he said.

"I'm sorry."

"I knew I couldn't out there. I thought maybe in here."

He had a quick low funny little laugh that ended almost every sentence he spoke. It was infectious, made me smile.

"I had to step out twice to have a butt before I came in. Wendy held my place."

"I'd like to let you." Another lie. "But we have a lot of sick people here."

How could he ever think I'd let him smoke in that room?

"My problem is really, really embarrassing. I told the tall woman I had stomach problems, but that isn't it. I'm sorry, I lied. My problem is that I can't get it up."

That was a first.

"Don't worry, dude, I don't want you to touch it." That crazy laugh again. "It's also kind of small, which is another problem. I just, like, wondered if you could do anything."

I shrugged. "I never know."

"Please don't prescribe meditation. I don't think that'll cut it."

That goofy laugh again. I couldn't help smiling.

"That's what you often suggest, people say. It ain't for me. Unless I can sit there smoking."

More and more I was talking about zazen, especially to the gringos. They came to Julie's when they should have come to the zendo. There was a spiritual problem beneath the physical. For that I had one answer.

"So how did this come about?" I said. "Did something happen?"

"No, dude, nothing. That's the whole problem."

That laugh again. This guy was terminally embarrassed.

"Just kidding. It's not like I've never done the deed. I have. But I was with this girl I really liked—I mean, of all the people for it to happen with."

"That's exactly who it does happen with."

"It's not like there was no reaction, but it was pretty limp. I tried to get in and couldn't, then it deflated completely. Since then, nothing. Almost like it gets smaller."

"How did she respond?"

"She was great. Said it was no big deal. It'd come around. But it was so fucking embarrassing. I couldn't go on."

"You stopped seeing her?"

"I'm afraid to see anybody. Afraid she told somebody, though I don't think she would."

"Never."

"There's only so much humiliation you can take. I'm in a bad spot."

"This has happened to me."

"I know man, but you're, like, old."

"When I was young. It happens to everybody."

"I've heard that before, but I'm between a rock and a hard place, oh shit. Unfortunate choice of words."

He was as embarrassed to be alive as Wendy was ashamed to be alive.

"I won't prescribe meditation."

"Thanks, dude. And please don't touch my thing, if you could even find it right now, I'm so nervous. I'm like homophobic out the wazoo. Oops. Another great word choice."

That laugh again. I had to laugh myself.

"But when I do fix this up," I said. "Which I will. When this whole thing is a bad memory, I want you to try meditation. Because it's good for what ails you. Even this."

He did show up at the zendo, a week later. Gave me a big thumbs-up as he walked in.

"The problem isn't with your cock," I said.

"I know, man. I'm a champ when I'm alone."

"Sex is an energy. Starts in your balls and runs through your whole body, cycles around. It's sexual energy, spiritual energy, whatever. It's everything."

"Yeah. Right. Maybe."

"The problem is when it gets stuck somewhere. That can happen different places. Yours is stuck here."

I touched his heart.

"How do you know?"

"I can see energy."

That was bullshit, but it sounded good.

"I'm going to touch you here." I kept one hand on his heart, put the other at the same spot on his back, so I cupped his heart. "Try to pull your shoulders back. Open up."

He was not good at that.

"The mistake you made was leaving that girl. How did you really feel about her?"

"I loved her. I still love her." His voice cracked.

"Did you tell her?"

"That was for after. There was no after."

"Tell her before. Go back to her and tell her why you stopped seeing her. You couldn't do it because you loved her. You wanted it too much."

"That's God's truth."

"Tell her you love her. That's the only important thing. Fucking isn't important. Love is. But when you get that in place, everything will follow."

"I don't know if I can do this."

"You can. Anybody can. Do just like I told you. No matter how nervous you are."

"I'll be shitting bricks."

"She won't care. She'll love it. I guarantee it."

He did seem encouraged.

And don't laugh like that! Not after every sentence, I wanted to say, but didn't.

The young man looked a little shaky when he walked out but seemed determined.

Now go out there and get a hard-on!

The next person who stepped in—the biggest surprise of the day, if not the whole summer—was Stone Rockwell. The bald dome with the stringy hair down his back, huge beer belly, cavernous hollows under his eyes: He looked every bit the whipped basset hound, blushing fiercely. He sat down with a thump.

"You're surprised to see me," he said.

"A little. Always a pleasure."

What a liar I'd become.

"I came for your blessing."

Great God.

"I don't do many blessings, Stone."

"I just mean ... I want to apologize. I've been bad-mouthing you. Even to your son."

"He likes the negative stuff. Thinks it gives him credibility."

"I hope to Christ he won't use it."

"I think he will."

"Oh, hell."

"But I know one thing. It's no use trying to persuade him, one way or another. He's stubborn as a mule."

He'd been that way since he was a kid.

"I felt like you invaded my turf. I had a healing practice first."

"I didn't mean to. Never intended this at all."

"I said you weren't qualified. Hadn't put in the years learning bodywork."

"Perfectly true."

"Said you didn't know what you were doing. You just have this freak gift."

"True again."

"But that story of the mother you made fertile. The little Mexican couple. I don't often cry at the news. But that had me bawling like a baby."

After how many beers?

"My hat's off to you, man. You've got something."

It cost Stone something to say that. His mouth was pursed and trembling, eyes sad.

"I wish I had a tiny piece of it."

I looked into those sad eyes, facing this perpetual mystery.

"Do you think it really happened?" I said.

"The girl is pregnant."

"We know how that happens."

"They'd been banging away for years. She felt something change when you touched her."

"I have a feeling it was her, somehow."

"You never take credit. You've got to get over that."

"You have a tangible skill. Cure someone's back pain or something. I just touch them. Don't know what I'm doing. Something happens or it doesn't."

"You've got this power in your hands. Can you give it to me?"

There were times I gladly would have.

The face I was staring at was terribly sad, those cavernous eyes, down-turned mouth. He looked like he was hanging on the edge of a cliff. About two inches from being a total barfly.

"I know you don't want to hear this," I said. "I really think zazen is the way."

"I know you do. But I'm an old man. Don't have that kind of time."

He was probably younger than me.

"Just bless me, Hank. Please. Bless me."

I put my hands on his shoulders. Never in my life had I felt like such a total fraud.

"I can feel it," he said. "Christ, I can feel it."

His face lit up. He actually smiled, first time I'd seen that. He looked good when he smiled.

"Thank you, Hank. Really. You don't know what this means."

"Come to the zendo, Stone. Sit like a rock."

He even had me making stupid jokes.

"I will, Hank. You'll see me there. You'll see me this week."

We never did see him, alas. What we did see, the next week, was an ad on the back page of the local weekly. *Hands Blessed by Henry Wilder. Bodywork with a Difference. Come to the Rock and Find Strength. Stone Rockwell.*

"I can't believe the gall of the man," Julie said when she saw it.

"He's all gall," I said.

*

Padre Roberto had been out of town ever since that Mass where I'd been recognized, had gone to see his parents. He'd thought he'd see me that day after Mass.

"But you took off like a bat out of hell," he said, with a big grin.

"It was just so embarrassing."

"I had no idea Luis could give such a talk. He has a real flare."

One of his parishioners, a woman who owned a taco stand, had gotten word of our lunches and of Padre's feeling he should contribute. She said she would furnish the food. She made tortas, the massive sandwiches that Mexicans fill with everything under the sun, then defy you to eat without spilling the ingredients all over yourself.

"These are *milanesa*," he said. "The crème de la crème. Her son just brought them over."

We were meeting at my house, sitting at the dining room table. I furnished Negra Modelo. I thought that a step up from the Especial.

My torta would have served three people. Padre Roberto didn't look even slightly daunted.

"So what did you make of his story?" I said.

"The crowd thought it was a miracle."

"That's not what I asked."

The food was delicious. I was glad we didn't meet every day.

"Getting pregnant is a mystery. You hear about people trying and trying, not being able to. Finally they adopt, and the woman gets pregnant that week."

"Right."

"It's something to do with how receptive the woman is. In some totally mysterious way."

"I never heard of such a young girl being told she couldn't get pregnant."

"You've got to wonder where that was. What kind of doctor."

"There was also an American doctor. Someone around here."

"We could talk to him. I have a feeling it wouldn't help."

He was moving through that torta the way I put down a peanut butter cracker. The Negra Modelo went in about four gulps.

"Another beer?" I said.

"Maybe some water. I'm planning to work out."

Wouldn't want to be too full.

"She came to my office and told me about this," he said. "Long before Luis gave his talk. She felt something move inside her, when you touched her."

"I think it was her faith."

"She thinks it was your hands. I think it was beyond both of you."

Catholics love that kind of talk.

"Why is this happening to me, Padre?"

"Don't take it personally. It's just happening. It's a good thing."

"I don't like the new direction."

I told him about people who came to see me. The hypochondriacs, the kid who couldn't get it up. Stone Rockwell, for God's sake (his ad hadn't appeared yet, or I'd have gone berserk). All kinds of people who wanted some vaguely spiritual experience.

"People are coming to Julie's who should come to the zendo. Think if I touch them they'll get zapped with thirty years of Zen training."

"Make them come to the zendo."

"I do. But there's a gray area, like the thing with Stone. The easier thing, the quicker one, is just to touch him. Then I feel bad afterwards, like a snake-oil salesman."

"All you do is your best. Use your best judgment."

"Time is short. People are outside the door. I'm in there trying to help some kid get a hard-on."

"I can't think of a more compassionate act. Except helping me not get one." He laughed.

For that he had to touch himself.

"A priest faces lots of what you're asking," he said. "But beyond your notions of what's important, of what's authentic, everybody's suffering. The hypochondriacs. Stone. You don't know what to do. You don't always do the right thing. But everybody deserves your compassion. And whatever help you can give them."

That brought me up short.

"The Mexicans seem different," I said.

He smiled. "They do. But you mean Latinos."

"I might. But I might just mean Mexicans. There's something about them. That Virgin."

"There's definitely something about the Virgin."

"They don't come with trivialities. They're not concerned with stupid things. Their lives are real."

"We're seeing a small part of the population. Ones who come here to help their families. They're brave and resourceful."

"And happen to be taking a lot of shit."

"True. I have this struggle of my own. Would rather work with them. I've always felt that way. For my own development I should probably be with conservatives in the Midwest. Eating tuna noodle casserole. But the Church needs me here. I know the culture. Speak the language."

He sure as hell ate the food.

"So I get to work with the people I love," he said.

"They have a kind of faith other people don't," I said.

"They've had to, to do what they've done."

"It's hard to put your finger on."

"I don't know if you've read the history of Mexican religion. The cathedrals were built on ruins of Indian temples. Sometimes the Indians who built them hid messages to their gods."

I hadn't known that.

"Those people don't worry about Catholic theology. What they have is an utter faith that whatever happens, God is with them. The Virgin cradles them in her arms. In that way they don't care. They've given up completely."

It was the way we were supposed to give ourselves up in Zen. These people just did it.

*

I lay in bed with Julie that evening. It was the place we did most of our talking those days, we were so busy.

"I'm fascinated by this devotion the Mexicans have," I said.

I was on my back and she on her side, rubbing my belly.

"You seem devoted," she said. "Devout. Whatever the word is."

"I try."

"Wasn't Jake devoted?"

"Utterly. Through and through. But these folks are devoted to a person. An image."

"Which represents a value. That maternal spirit. Compassion and love."

We had the same image in Buddhism, in the Metta Sutra, where we chanted, "Even as a mother protects with her life / Her child, her only child, /So with a boundless heart/ Should one cherish all living beings." Somehow, in Zen, that didn't seem central.

"It has a warmth Zen doesn't," I said.

"Wasn't Jake warm?"

"Very."

"You're warm. Don't worry about warmth."

"I'm getting hot at the moment."

How could rubbing somebody's belly be erotic? It was when Julie did it.

"The trouble with Zen is when people think they're working on themselves," I said. "To become enlightened."

"And the problem with Catholicism is when people rub some beads and think everything will be all right."

"Everything *will* be all right."

"Not the way they mean. Every religion is strong here and weak there. I still believe what that Korean master said. All religions converge at one point."

Maybe my problem was that the sangha was so young. I didn't have the senior students Jake had. Julie was an exception, mature on her own.

People were asking where the healing power came from, as if that were a goal.

"You look tired." Julie touched her hand to my face.

"I'm in the right place then."

"Deeply tired. I used to have a feeling, when I gave you a massage, that I got the stress out. You took stuff in every day and I got it out. I don't have that feeling now."

I was worn out. Hadn't been sleeping well.

"Sometimes I want to tell every gringo at the clinic to get the hell out of there," I said. "Quit feeling sorry for themselves and practice zazen. Practice something. They've turned me into a therapist."

"I know."

"Though they already have one. If not two or three."

Yet people were suffering, as Padre Roberto said.

"Sooner or later they'll figure out I can't zap their problems away. I'll be one more fad that didn't work."

"I hope."

"And I'll start to get some sleep."

In the back of both of our minds was the approaching school year. We'd promised to make a decision on that by August first, also vowed not to talk about it before then. It would have taken up every evening.

At that point, I couldn't imagine walking away.

FIFTEEN

Josh and I were sitting in my living room; he had come over to show me more clips. That seemed to be the only way I saw him. The people he interviewed were available only in the evenings or on weekends, and he spent hours going through his clips, imagining how things would work together. He'd never done a documentary before.

He actually looked strung out, though there was no deadline that I knew of.

"That incident at the church changed everything," he said. "Created a new movie. I wish you'd thought to take me to that."

"I don't think of filming in a church."

"There's a way to be discreet. Which reminds me. I need to do some shots at the new zendo. See this larger group."

"It may not be larger for long. People come and go."

"Meg says it's dramatic. An entirely different feel to chanting."

It made a difference to have a lot of voices. An experienced core.

"I didn't know that Mass would be such a big deal," I said. "Had no idea."

"That's the new center of the film, no question. I've started over."

"What about Esmeralda? The old guy with arthritis?"

"They'll be in it. I don't see them as central."

Esmeralda? Not central?

"That doesn't sound right."

"I want to hear your opinion. But have a look at what I've got."

He pushed a button and up popped Stone Rockwell, the first time I'd ever seen him that he didn't look terminally hungover.

"Good Lord. Is he wearing makeup?"

"Not that I put on him."

"He looks like a new man."

"Just listen."

"It changed my mind about everything," Stone said. "I was at the point of calling your father a fake. I'm afraid you've still got that footage." He grinned, almost boyishly. "But that story changed me. Moved from bodywork to the deeply spiritual. Though I think bodywork *is* spiritual."

The clip jumped.

"That's still rough," Josh said. "It'll look better."

"I think it changed your father too," he said. "Left him in awe of what he'd done."

"That's ridiculous, Josh."

"We'll cut things. But one of my ideas is to see that Mass as a turning point, after which nothing is the same. We'd start with the boy whose leg you healed. Talk to some minor people."

"Minor?"

"The old guy with arthritis. The muscle aches. I've got fifteen or twenty of those, all Latino. Shots of the old zendo. Then we'd jump to the new one. And feature clips like this."

He called up another image. Great God. It was Whiny Wendy.

"Where did you find her?"

"Friend of Meg's. Called me up."

She too looked different, had let her hair out, so it hung to her shoulders. Her face, which had been tight with tension, looked bright and clear. She was smiling, as Stone had been. No wonder I didn't recognize them.

"She's definitely made up," I said.

"She must have done it herself. Listen."

"I wanted him to touch my stomach. The same way he touched that *beautiful* Mexican woman. Wanted to feel what she had felt."

She seemed animated, alive, had a sparkle in her eyes. I would almost have called her pretty. What happened?

"I have trouble with my intestines," she said. "Don't like to talk about it. I should say *had* troubles." Big smile. "I definitely needed healing."

She looked like a different person.

"That woman said she felt something shift. *Shift* for me was hardly the term," she continued. "It was a total transformation. As if the molecules dissolved and took new form. The energy was astounding. I've been to bodyworkers, chiropractors, cranial sacral. I've never felt anything like it in my life."

"The Mexican people spoke haltingly," Josh said. "There's the whole problem of subtitles and voiceovers. This is so vivid. Like good fiction."

"It *is* good fiction."

"She's convincing, Dad. You're not giving her a chance."

"I've gone to zazen," Wendy said. "Haven't gotten the hang of it. It seems kind of, I don't know, I hate to say it, boring." A high titter. "That isn't your father's true mission. Healing is the center of who he is."

"Josh ..."

"We can cut it. She's just yacking."

"Is there more?"

"We could sit here for a couple of hours."

145

I'd better make him stop before he showed me a kid sitting there with a hard-on.

"I've been working hard, Dad. This is the tip of the iceberg."

I'd never been one to criticize my son's work. It didn't seem my place. Particularly not in this case.

"The last time we talked this seemed completely different," I said, "focused on what I would call true healing. Esmeralda was at the heart."

"She could still be important."

"That was still the most touching story I've heard."

"I have Luis and Hortensia on film for a full half hour. They talk about what this meant to their lives. To their faith."

"Esmeralda is the real thing."

"How is becoming fertile not the real thing?"

"Josh. People fuck. They have a baby. It's a miracle. It might be the greatest miracle in the universe. But I don't bring it about."

"You brought this about. They're convinced."

"There's no way you'll prove it. The situation with Esmeralda is deeper."

"I don't see it that way."

"She's not claiming a miracle. She knows she's going to die. But her attitude has changed. Her life has changed."

"She's also a professor. She's been in this country twenty years. She doesn't represent your people."

"Neither does Wendy."

Maybe she did, more and more.

"Luis and Hortensia are the emotional heart. Any story-teller would say that. I don't see why you don't see it."

"I don't know if I did anything for them."

"You keep saying that. But you welcomed them into your office, whatever you call that place. You listened to her talk, whether you understood or not. You put your hand on her belly. Now she's pregnant. Those are facts."

Josh when he was sure of himself spoke in a different way. When he'd arrived at my place he looked like a harried caffeine crazed film director, saying anything that sounded good. On this point he spoke with conviction.

"Listen, Dad. Nobody on the face of the earth has been more skeptical of this whole thing than I have. I don't even believe in zazen, for Christ's sake. I sometimes wish you were still a history teacher. But something happened. Person after person confirmed it. You touched Hortensia and something moved inside her. She's not a flake. She's not an airhead."

"Wendy's an airhead."

"We'll leave Wendy out. Or just give her a sentence or two. I'm not making final cuts. I'm sketching a shape."

"I liked it when Esmeralda was the center."

"Most people will see Esmeralda as a failure."

"She's the one person who got the whole thing."

Josh shut down his laptop. He took a long drink from his coffee, ran his hand through his hair.

"I can see that. She represents an important part of this that I shouldn't leave out. Maybe I overreacted. But she's a kind of aristocrat. A professor, not the people you see day in and day out. Who are going to touch people's hearts and bring them to this film."

"I thought she was touching."

"Luis and Hortensia are illegal."

"You know that?"

"I haven't asked. It's obvious. He does construction work, she cleans houses. For them to step forward in this situation and go public was a big deal. It was dangerous. They still wanted to. That's how much they believe in it."

"You're going to say that?"

"I'm going to make it so obvious I don't need to. The heart of this story, the emotional heart, is poor people coming to this country to help their families. The way Latinos value family above everything. They even give God a mother. These Latino Catholics come to a Buddhist priest who happens to have an image of the Virgin. Doesn't even know what it means."

"True."

"It's a story about immigrants and about family. At the heart of it is an event that Luis and Hortensia call a miracle."

"We won't use that term."

"You'll never hear me say it. But I have to let them. I think something happened. Which is a long way from where I started."

He began getting together his things, stood up. He had another interview.

"I still don't know how I'm going to do all this. Frame the movie as a whole. Less and less am I thinking it's about me, even about you. But it's nice to have found its heart. That's a wonderful moment."

He finished his coffee, tossed the cup at a wastebasket across the room. Swish. The kid couldn't miss.

"Unless you pull off another miracle," he said. "Then it's back to the drawing board."

"I'll try to hold off."

We had stepped onto the porch. Another muggy day.

"I thought I was going to see you all the time down here," I said.

"I thought I'd see you too. I have to get in line. Have some ailment."

"For you there's no charge."

"I'll try to come up with something. I still want to do that interview."

"Do it sooner rather than later."

"Really? Why?"

"Just do it sooner."

*

I'd been wanting to make the trip for some time, now had an excuse. I called that afternoon and after initially being flustered, she said she'd be happy to see me. She gave me directions involving beltlines and various streets with British names. I've always found Raleigh a strange place.

The thing that strikes me is that no matter what part of town I'm in, it all looks the same. The wide highways packed with cars, strip malls of all shapes and sizes, the generic chain restaurants, car dealers, pet superstores. Yep, I'm in Raleigh. The old downtown has its charm, like all the Southern cities that have been renovated, but what's grown up around it is hideous.

She lived in what is known as a town home, near the university. It was decent looking, almost new. She opened the door right after I rang, dressed in a scarlet blouse and black skirt, a patterned shawl over her shoulders. If anything, she was more beautiful in person than on the screen.

"Hank. Come in."

"So nice of you to have me, Esmeralda."

It was a shock after the suburban front, bland houses all around; her house was a profusion of color. The living room was not decorated, I would say, but jammed with Mexican art. It was overwhelming.

"Wow." I took a couple of steps in.

"It's too much for some people. I've been collecting for years. It wasn't quite so crowded before my divorce, when I was downtown, and the house was larger."

There were paintings all over the walls, arranged by artist. There were small dolls, *animalitos*, religious icons, cards. We walked around the ground floor and saw the full range. I'd never seen anything like it.

"I love the art of my country," she said. "The colors. I find the US colorless. Like all these houses." She nodded toward the outside.

The place was beautiful, but I couldn't stop staring at her.

"I made some limeade," she said. "But I could also make you a real Margarita. Hard to get in this country."

"I have to drive."

"I know. Or I would have made them already. Also, I didn't know if Buddhists drink."

"Real ones don't. I do. I'll have one if you will."

"That's wonderful. We'll celebrate your visit."

She stepped to the small bar in her living room and got to work.

"Some bartenders say the salt on the glass is to hide the taste of bad tequila. But I kind of like the salt. Do you have a preference?"

"Whatever you say." I hesitated. "I've actually never had a Margarita."

"Your first Margarita. What an occasion. It's like taking a virgin." She laughed.

She worked slowly and carefully, first squeezing limes. I walked around looking at the art.

"I'll be gentle," she said.

"Where did you get all this?"

"All over Mexico. Different things in different places. There's a long lecture, which I'll spare you. I bring my classes here."

She walked over with our glasses. "But they get the limeade. *Salud*. To your health."

"And yours." I said it without thinking.

She nodded. "Thank you."

She sat on a small couch, I on a chair facing it.

"I'm so glad we had a chance to meet," she said, "in this other context. I don't know if you remember me. Speaking Spanish as if it was all I knew."

"I remember."

I could never forget a woman so beautiful.

It seemed strange to say, especially for a Buddhist, but I couldn't believe, staring at her, that she was going to die.

"I noticed that art in the corner," I said.

She had a whole collection of skulls, painted and elaborately decorated. Around them on the wall were drawings of skeletons.

"It's a tradition to make fun of death in Mexico," she said. "To see it everywhere, in everything you do." One of the drawings was of bride and groom skeletons. She also had a small toy, little skeletons fucking.

"That permeates the culture," she said, "but it's theoretical. Something like this happens"—she touched her chest—"and you see the truth of it."

There was something absolutely calm about her, like a woman on her deathbed.

"That's like Buddhism," I said.

"I've noticed. It's something about indigenous people everywhere."

"You must wonder why I came."

"I'm very happy you came."

"I saw the interview you did with my son."

"You have a handsome, intelligent son."

I nodded, smiled. "I've seen various interviews. Somehow, watching yours, I saw what my work is all about."

She nodded, paused for a moment.

"The person is healed, though they're no better," she said.

"There may be different kinds of healing. But we know yours was real, because you didn't get anything tangible."

She nodded. "I got the better thing. But I heard about the woman you ... made pregnant." She laughed. "That's not the way to say that. But that's wonderful. That you were able to help her."

"People come to me every day. They talk to me and I touch them. I try to listen, try really to touch. Don't know if I've done a thing."

"You have."

"But I don't know how. Don't know why. I don't know how I got into all this."

She laughed.

"Many of the others only speak Spanish," I said. "They also talk in this other idiom. It's not just the Spanish. It's a way of talking."

"*The Virgin will help me.*"

"Yes."

"Would you like to see my Virgins? They're upstairs."

We went up a narrow stairway to the second floor. There were two bedrooms up there. One was entirely devoted to the collection of Virgins, which was spectacular. She had statues of all shapes and sizes, as well as framed images on the wall. It was amazing how varied they were.

"I used to have these in different places," she said. "But I pulled them together."

"They're beautiful."

"This is the most cherished image in our culture. Also a symbol of female power and grace. I've collected them for years. This is my refuge."

In the middle of the room was a meditation place, a *zabuton* and a *zafu*.

"These are the new additions," she said. "I arranged the room around them. With them I'm not so familiar."

"I have a collection of them."

"My thoughts as I sit are quite persistent."

"That tends to be true."

"They're all about death. I sit here and wait to die." She smiled. "I know that sounds morbid. I don't mean it that way. But I need to remember."

"We all need to. Most people don't remind themselves."

We walked back downstairs, sat again in the living room

"How's your first Margarita?"

"Wonderful. I could learn to like this."

"Don't like it too much." She smiled, took a sip. "I'm so glad you came. I wanted to talk to you. But I was a little shy, especially after pretending only to speak Spanish. I hoped you would see that interview."

"It was one of the first things Josh showed me."

She started to talk about her life, told me she had been born in Guadalajara, the second-largest city in Mexico. "Mexico City is a huge international city, like New York or London. Guadalajara is also huge, but completely Mexican."

Her father had been in real estate, eventually owned one of the largest hotels in town. She went to a private school where they spoke Spanish in the morning and English in the afternoon, grew up completely bilingual. Her father thought that essential. She traveled a great deal as a girl, grew enchanted with the United States, especially the West Coast. When it came time to choose a college, she went to UCLA.

"My father's idea was that I would attend this gringo college and go back to Guadalajara. But I'd seen so many people go back and get shitty jobs, way below what they could do. Women especially. Smart women. Employment is *so* difficult in Mexico."

She studied Spanish literature with the goal of becoming a professor in this country. She got her PhD at UCLA as well, hoped to teach on the West Coast. But the job market was terrible. First she went to the University of Rochester, then wound up at North Carolina State.

"I encountered huge amounts of prejudice. Against Latinos. Women. Attractive Latino women. People thinking I couldn't possibly be intelligent. Men, on the other hand, were certain I'd like to screw my way up the academic ladder. I also found myself in these situations where I'd walk into a room and people would think I was there to clean up or something. Some of it was funny, but I felt a lot of rage. My antidote was to drink Tequila." She raised her glass. "And suck in smoke."

She shook her head. "I'm not saying prejudice led to my illness. We all smoked in Mexico when I was young. But I do associate my anger with addiction, that feeling of sucking in something harsh to match the harshness inside, swallowing rage and trying to be calm.

"I'm almost glad I'm sick because it made me give up smoking. Made me face my rage instead of tamping it down."

She took a long sip from her drink.

"Sometimes I think I gave up all the good and beautiful things in my country in pursuit of success. Does this look like success to you?"

I shrugged. "It could be worse."

"It wasn't what I hoped for."

The academic ladder was endless. Seldom had I met anyone who was happy with where they wound up.

"I must look like a religious person, with all my Virgins. But it was really the art that enchanted me. The beautiful colors and simple faith of my people. I studied religion like other subjects in my life, took it on as an intellectual endeavor. Catholic theology is so elaborate. I couldn't swallow it."

That was the way Christianity had been for me. I had gotten caught up in the theory, never got to the heart.

"That left me without much recourse when I got ill. I started attending Mass again, still wasn't getting much.

"I can't possibly explain what it was for me to see you. Seeing that woman on television, whose son you healed. Hearing the Latino people talk."

"It was a moving show."

"It was as if I were giving in to something. Doing something I would never have done in my country. Associating with a kind of people—it wasn't that I scorned them. I loved them. But I had tried to get away from all that, what I saw as mumbo jumbo and superstition. Become a professor in the gringo world.

"So it was terribly moving. All these little women with their baskets of food. The stories of their illnesses, and all the other hardships. It broke my heart, in a good way. When they heard I had cancer, they were all over me. Crying, crossing themselves. They were sure you would help me. You had a Virgin in your office, they kept saying."

"If it weren't for that, none of this would have happened."

"I was still half expecting some quack who had figured out a way to take advantage of Latino people. At least someone who would try to impress me. But you listened calmly to all I said, your eyes so sad. I don't want this to sound wrong, but I don't know how else to put it: You didn't seem like a gringo."

Sounded like a compliment.

"It was terribly powerful when you touched me. Awkward, because you didn't want to touch my breasts. You put one hand between them, the other on my back. I didn't feel the power everyone talks about, and the energy. I did cry. Do you remember?"

"I do."

"What I felt was love. That whole morning was love. Those women as I waited, your assistant when she spoke to me, you as you listened. But when you touched me it was completely different, a love I'd never felt before. It wasn't for me. It wasn't from you. It was just love, all around. All the things that stood in my way in the Catholic Church fell away. They didn't matter anymore. This was what it was about. This was what everybody was talking about. I could go to Mass, take the Eucharist. I could also not do that. It was all love.

"And I asked, I don't know if you remember, but I asked afterwards where you found this power. You told me all you did was sit. Everything came from sitting. I decided that day that I would try. It's the same as praying, I think."

"I agree."

"Because who needs words? There are no words for what I felt that day. Love doesn't begin to say it."

I'd had the experience Esmeralda was talking about, that sudden uprushing of love. That's the rock-bottom place, when you finally get to the heart of everything, just love, overwhelming in its power, though it isn't the bottom of anything; it opens out into everything, infinitely. It doesn't come from somewhere, like when you wonder where something comes from. It just is, everywhere.

"So I can sit upstairs with my Virgins," Esmeralda said. "I can sit with the little group I found here in Raleigh, which meets in somebody's house. I can go to Mass, sit there. I don't know if I'm meditating, praying, or what. It doesn't matter. I go to the Kroger afterwards, and it's the same there. The whole world is different. I'm so grateful."

"But you know it wasn't me. You understand that."

"You set up a situation. It might never have happened otherwise."

"The problem is when someone thinks it's me."

"I don't think anyone would feel that way who this happened to."

"It doesn't happen to too many people."

"Which is why I'm so lucky. Even having cancer."

"I worry that I'm in the way, for some people."

"In the way?"

"If they think it's me, they'll never see the truth."

*

"I bet you wanted to fuck her," Julie said. "She's so beautiful."

"This wasn't the kind of conversation you fuck somebody
after."

"I mean before that. When she gave you the Margarita.
What was that all about?"

"Not what you're thinking."

"You were her savior."

"She knows better than that. Besides. You don't want to
fuck your savior, do you?"

"I don't know what I'm doing here then."

We were in bed, in the dark. It was one of our presleep
conversations.

"You're my woman," I said. "You've always been my woman.
We have karma."

"We do."

"Even before I knew what karma was."

It was funny to think of all the ways we'd known each other,
the different things we'd been. What we were now.

"You've done as much for me as I did for you," I said.
"Healed me of that attachment to sex."

"You were already healed."

"But you showed me I could go back. I didn't have to be
afraid of it."

"You of all people were never afraid of sex."

"You showed me I wouldn't fall back into that old way I was."

I believe she had done it consciously. Brought me along slowly. She was a healer.

"That was no excuse to go off and fuck Esmeralda."

"I didn't. I wouldn't think of it."

The jealousy of women has no bounds. At least this woman.

I lay with my head on her shoulder, rubbed her belly, the way she often rubbed mine. It was a cure-all.

"I think I should disappear for a while," I said.

"How do you mean?"

"Fall off the face of the earth. Vanish."

"Why?"

"The fact that I'm here keeps people from seeing the point."

"Explain it to them."

"They don't hear it. I'm the one person they can't get it from."

"You have to figure this out. How to explain it."

"I can't do it. I'm stupid."

I felt that way sometimes.

"Where would you go?"

"I have an idea. But I don't want to say. So no one will know."

"You did fuck her. You just don't want to tell me. You're running away with her."

"Julie. Listen. Stone doesn't need me to bless his hands. He needs to get out of the bars and discover his healing power. It's not a technique. It's there."

"Stone's a nitwit."

"Whiny Wendy doesn't need to come to me week after week, thinking she'll be okay if I touch her. She needs to discover the health in her. That she already has."

"You're picking great examples."

"There are lots of people like that."

"Who's going to run the zendo?"

"You are. You've been running it for weeks."

"I've been practicing Zen exactly two months."

"You're not going to be the teacher. You'll just see that the bells get rung. The chanting gets done. Or skip the chanting. Just do the sitting. See who stays."

"What about the clinic?"

"You can do that. You're a healer."

"Not like you."

"Close enough. Listen. The Mexicans know it's the Virgin. They'll keep coming. The little group will still be there, of people who wait in line and talk to each other and share food. Listen to what they say, touch them, let them pray to the Virgin and meet a friendly gringo. The same thing will happen."

"I don't believe that."

"Then it won't. The people will stop coming. You'll have your bodywork business. Your Zen practice."

"Why would you do this, when things are going so well? People are devoted to you. You're finally successful. I wanted this for you."

"I appreciate that."

"You're throwing it away."

"Julie. Listen. What if I died?"

"Why would you die?"

"If things keep going this way, it's going to kill me. They'll make a reality TV show out of me and I'll die on the air."

"What about Josh's movie?"

"He's got enough. He's interviewing me tomorrow. Besides. This isn't the movie he should have made. He needs to move on. He should have stayed in that stuck place until something came up."

"Are you coming back?"

"At some point, when the dust has settled, I'll come back. To the three people who are still sitting with you. That'll be the group. I'll be their teacher. We'll grow it the right way."

Julie shook her head.

"I won't touch anybody," I said.

"You better touch me."

"I will. I'll touch you whenever you want."

I touched a place she especially liked.

"The other thing is," I said, "there's something I want to see. Something I need to understand."

"Can't you take me with you?"

"You've got to stay here. And I've got to go alone. You already know this thing anyway."

"And you're not going to tell me where."

"I'll tell you if you want. Before I leave. If you decide you want to know."

SIXTEEN

In the next day's mail I got a letter from the principal of my high school. He had considered the matter for a number of weeks and decided reluctantly that he couldn't ask me back for the following year. I'd been a wonderful teacher for them, but all the publicity surrounding my other activities had created a problem.

"Frankly," the letter said, "your work as a Zen teacher had always been a touchy point, but we overlooked it when it was minor." When no one actually attended. "As you know, we have a strongly Christian community. Your work as a New Age Shaman"—ouch—"has upset a number of our parents. I hope you'll agree that your resignation is best for all concerned."

"Is this a shock?" Josh said when he was setting up for our interview.

"Not really. I figured I wasn't going back. Just couldn't pull the trigger."

"What'll you do for money?"

"Money is in abundance at the moment. We'll see."

I hadn't told him of my plans. Hadn't told anyone but Julie.

"I hate to see a great teacher go down the tubes," he said.

"Things can change. Somebody might have me."

"Friends School is your only shot. But you'd have to teach an elective in New Age Shamanism."

That would be tough.

"So how will we do this?" Josh said. "You want to sit on a chair or your cushion?"

"I can think better on the cushion."

Josh frowned. "Honestly, Dad."

"There's something to it. The posture."

"So why don't we do it in the meditation room? I'll be on that same level, with the camera. We'll make it look as natural as possible."

I had one small room that was entirely devoted to sitting, though I hardly sat there anymore, what with everything at the zendo. I was never much of one for statues or altars but did have relics from twenty years of practice. One of my favorites was a reclining laughing Hotei (the fat Chinese Buddha) given to me by a Chinese waitress friend. Another was a standing fat Buddha, carved out of wood, that came from Korea. I tended to like fat Buddhas because they suggested abundance and good nature. They also reminded me of Jake (who wasn't *that* fat).

"I don't know how many times we may have to talk," Josh said.

"I wouldn't count on many. I'm a busy man."

"I wasn't thinking once would get it done."

"I'd try to get it covered today."

I didn't tell him that was all we had. Didn't want to make him nervous.

"All right," he said when he was finally set up. I was holding the wooden Buddha in my hand, rubbing its belly. "Let's just do a sound check. State your name."

"Henry Wilder. Hank, they call me."

"The Hammer. Your age?"

"Fifty-nine. Soon to turn sixty."

"It's scary. My father's an old man."

My son had a receding hairline. *That* was scary.

"So I'd just like, as much as possible," Josh said. "I say this to everybody, though it'll be harder for you. I'd like you to forget any conversations we've ever had. Forget who I am. I'd like you to try to be completely open to the questions. Answer with the first thing that comes to mind. That makes the best answer."

There was something Zen about that.

"Don't worry about verbal slips. Saying something you'll regret later. That's what editing is for."

"*I* don't get to edit."

"In this case you do. I'll show you everything before it's finished. Try to convince you that some totally inappropriate, basically moronic remark actually represents the true you, and needs to be in the film."

There was something to that.

"Anyway, let's get started."

I was holding the Buddha with my two hands, rubbing his belly with my thumbs. I could feel the sensation in *my* belly, somehow.

"When did you first feel you had healing powers?"

If Josh hadn't given me that pep talk, I would have said I didn't have healing powers. That's what I'd been saying to people for weeks, and it had its own kind of truth. But it was a defensive answer, didn't come from my deepest part.

"I've always felt I had healing powers," I said. "Ever since I was a kid. Once when I was lying on a couch with my father, your grandfather"—who died when I was sixteen, so Josh never met him—"he said, 'You have healing hands, Henry. The way your end fingers converge, as if they would meet at a point, those are healing hands.' He thought I should be a doctor. I had no idea where he got that."

"Why didn't you become a doctor?"

"I got a C in biology."

"And that was the end of that. So how did this other kind of healing get started?"

"In Zen we consider the lower abdomen an energy center. I don't know what a scientist would say, but to me that's a fact, from my experience. We also hold our hands at that spot, right down in front of the belly, in what we call the cosmic mudra." I put down the Buddha to demonstrate, left hand on top of right, thumb tips touching. "When I hold my hands that way, I feel energy move into them. I feel it in my whole body."

"You feel the energy as healing."

"All energy is healing, because it's energy. It's what makes you vital and alive."

"So that morning, when Julie told you her breast cancer had come back, where were you?"

"Whole Foods Café."

"And where did you do the healing?"

"We did it right there."

"You touched her breast in Whole Foods?"

"I touched both of them. Got the wrong one first."

"Dad...."

"You could take your clothes off and dance around in that place, nobody would even look up from their laptops. Guys probably feel up their girlfriends all the time."

"She wasn't your girlfriend."

She's been my girlfriend all along, I should have said. Forever. That's how I felt. But that would have freaked him out.

"That wasn't how it was. That's what I've tried to explain. If I could explain this one thing to people, I think the whole situation would make sense."

"So give it a try."

"Ever since Jake died, which happened a couple of years ago, I've felt myself gradually growing larger. Changing. As if his spirit had entered me."

Josh winced, but I had to go on. Julie would have understood.

"You could say it another way. The teacher died, and I took on the role, took on the responsibilities. I became larger in that way. But that's not the way it felt, from the inside. It was as if he were passing something on to me."

"All right."

"It didn't just happen when he died. It's continued for two years. It's still happening. That's what resurrection is. The teacher dies and the spirit passes into his followers. That's what happened with Jesus. Not to compare Jake to Jesus. But the disciples, who until then had seemed timid indecisive men, took on his spirit and acted as he had. It happened with the Buddha. He died and Ananda became enlightened."

"You could still see that as taking the role of teacher."

"Except that until recently, I hardly had any students, in Maine or down here. If you looked from the outside, I didn't look like a teacher."

"That was on the way. You were getting ready."

"*That* is a myth, as far as I'm concerned. It might never have happened. Could disappear in a puff of smoke right now. Anyway, Jake was a direct, open person. If somebody needed help, he helped. He saw what they needed and gave it to them. He didn't care how it looked, what conventions he was violating. One time he brought a homeless person into our house, gave him a bath, it took two rinses, bought him all new clothes at Goodwill. Made him dinner."

The guy subsequently drank every drop of liquor we had, but that was another story.

"Anyway, when I saw my old friend Julie in Whole Foods, Julie who had been my friend for years and once been my girlfriend, who told me her breast cancer had recurred, the first thing I said was, 'Can I touch it?' Which was entirely uncharacteristic of me. But at the same time was a natural response. A human response."

"Which most people wouldn't make."

"But in a natural world they would. It's an expression of compassion, an uprushing of love. I wouldn't say I did it. It just happened. I never decided to be a healer."

"But you touched her, and she was healed."

"I touched her and she doesn't have breast cancer at the moment. Other people I've touched still do have cancer."

"It doesn't always work."

"I don't know that it ever works. All I know are those two facts. I touched her and she doesn't have cancer. That's as far as I'll go."

We stopped for a moment. I was right at the heart of what I wanted to say.

"So how do you explain it?" Josh said.

"It was natural. Everything about it. Your friend comes to you with something wrong, something hurt, or some ill, and you do what you can, you listen to her, you touch her, in sympathy. You touch her where she hurts. It's a natural thing.

"Many of the people who come to me, who have problems with their shoulders, their necks, their stomachs, their backs, someone has listened to their symptoms. They've written prescriptions. They've used the best medical knowledge they have. But nobody has touched them. I'll touch a place and think, God, that's tight. It feels good for someone to put a hand on that."

"Many people report an extraordinary jolt of energy when you touch them. Your hands have an electric charge."

"Energy flows through human beings."

"Some more than others, it seems."

"In some people it gets stuck. Sometimes I think that's what illness is. Stuck energy. Other people don't feel the energy from another person. I'm not sure why. But some people are receptive, you can tell. It's like their bodies are more relaxed. Latino people are receptive."

"Why do you have this energy flow?"

"It may have developed out of my meditation practice, but that's natural too. Nothing could be more natural. To sit and feel the energy in your body. Look into yourself and see who you are, the way you're connected to everything around you. Call it meditation. Call it prayer. Call it sitting there. It's natural. But when people are strung out on caffeine, staring at their laptops, talking on their cell phones, sitting in a public place but not noticing life all around them, they don't see the woman crying. They don't find out she has cancer. They don't reach out and touch her. The energy doesn't flow."

"I don't understand how sitting makes the energy flow."

"I don't either. It just does, if I'm right about this. It's like an exercise I do with my students sometimes, especially beginners. I tell them to hold their hand out and give their complete attention to it. Or don't even hold it out. Pay attention, wherever it is. Sit and pay attention to your hand for four or five minutes. You begin to notice that it tingles. It's tingling. That's energy. It was there already, but you didn't notice because you weren't paying attention. You didn't create the energy. You just began to notice it. Meditation is like that. Only you pay attention to your whole body."

"I hate to be a skeptic, but I've done that a few times. I did it the first time you ever did, at Jake's, all those years ago. I didn't feel any energy."

"Neither did I. It takes a while. Months or years."

"Why would a person keep doing it if he doesn't feel anything?"

"Either you trust the person who's teaching you, figure it's got to be good if he's doing it, or you're totally desperate. You'll do anything. As Jake used to say when somebody left, 'Maybe they haven't suffered enough.'"

A certain kind of desperation was a help.

"You reverse an old pattern," I said. "A baby feels everything. You look at him lying there, jazzing around, and he's connected to the world. Completely open. But as we grow up we run into things that make us tighten. We don't like this or that, so we don't let it in. We close down. We have a whole lifetime of those things. That's the crap that comes up when we sit. It seems to be garbage. But in some way we have to let that come up, allow ourselves to see it, take it in. My father's death when I was sixteen was the hardest one for me. That came up in spades. But everything comes up. Your whole life passes before you.

"Somehow, over time, attention wears away that physical tension. Attention heals everything, Jake used to say. We get distracted by all the stuff that comes up, for a while that seems terribly important, all the content. But after a while we see it's just the same old crap, again and again, and come back to the body, which is infinitely interesting. It's utterly alive, becomes more and more open to the world. At some point, maybe, it's completely open. But I don't think the process of opening ever stops. It's a big world out there."

I had never said all this to anyone before, or maybe to Julie, in those early days when she kept questioning me. She soaked up everything. This was different. It was like telling the world.

"At some point you're energy and everybody else is energy. There's no distinction. The Zen teacher Eihei Dogen said as much, though he didn't use the word energy. But you're back to the baby situation, only taking a lot more in. That's how I used to think of Jake, as a great big baby. He was even bald. But totally articulate and intelligent. Full of love for everything."

"And you're at that point."

"I'm not."

"Then how can you heal people?"

"I have no idea. Don't know that I can. I happen to think it's all the Virgin. But I do know that something is seriously out of whack."

"How's that?"

"When people think the teacher is doing it. You have to come to the teacher. The teacher makes you whole. I don't know how I let this happen. Jake was never like this."

"He didn't have healing powers."

"Maybe he was just smart enough not to tell anybody."

He could heal just by listening to you.

"My intentions were good. Julie's were good. It seemed like a way to offer help to people who needed it. But then people are advertising that your hands blessed them."

"He's a nut."

"When they're getting you to touch them for the thrill of it. When somebody's making a movie—pardon me, Josh, if this had been anybody but my own son, I would have seen it long ago—when somebody's making a movie and people are coming to the zendo just to be in the movie, that's horseshit. It's out of balance. It's time to go."

"Go where?'

"That's between me and my priest."

That was a movie allusion. I wondered if he got it.

"Thank you, Ratso Rizzo."

He never missed.

"When?" he said.

"Saturday."

"*Sat*urday? Jesus Christ. When are you coming back?"

"I haven't decided. When things get back in balance."

I figured it would take a while. It had taken a while for them to get screwed up.

"I have to let people know this practice is about sitting. Them sitting, not me. That if the Virgin is going to heal, she can do it on her own. She doesn't need me."

"Maybe she wants you."

"Then she'll bring me back."

"I think the touching is important."

"They can touch each other."

"Dad...."

"Everybody's got the energy. The energy is everywhere. Of that I'm completely convinced. Besides. I thought you didn't believe in healing touch."

"You about had me convinced."

"It exists or it doesn't. It isn't me."

Josh looked crushed, completely despondent. He took it harder than Julie.

"I thought we were going to keep talking," he said.

"This is all I've got. I've told you everything."

"I'm right in the middle of the project."

"You've got what you need. I can see the movie right now."

I couldn't really, but felt sure he could, if he just looked.

Josh shook his head, ran his hand through his hair.

"I don't understand," he said. "You were finally a success. Beyond anything I ever imagined."

"This isn't success. This is failure. A total fuckup. I was doing better when I had two students up in Maine. When the teaching is right, the teacher disappears. My teaching at this point is all wrong. I'm a celebrity. I've got to really disappear."

*

My swim was late that afternoon. Never had it seemed more precious. I actually swam an extra quarter mile. If the place I was going didn't have a pool, I was in deep trouble. That was the most healing thing in my life.

The big black guy was in the locker room when I came out.

"Hey, man. I been looking for you. Can you give me one of them touches? Help me with my sugar?"

"You need to see a doctor."

"I did see a doctor."

"You got to quit eating so much junk."

"Shit, man. I know that."

"Why don't you do it?"

He shook his head, looked away. "Stupid motherfucker," he said.

I took the long way home, stopped by Immaculate Conception. Padre Roberto was in his office.

"Do you have a minute?" I said.

"Just. Evening Mass is about to begin."

"There's something I want to ask you."

*

That night in bed, Julie kept staring at me.

"Are you leaving forever?"

"I'll never leave you. We'll always be together. I'll be right here."

"It's not the same without the body." She was rubbing my belly. That was enough to make me stay. "The body is my favorite part."

"The body will follow. I swear."

"When you get there, call me. Don't tell me where if you don't want. Just call on your cell."

"Okay. But I don't want to talk too often. I need to really be gone."

"I know. You said that. I just need to know you're there."

She kept rubbing my belly. The woman knew what she was doing.

"God," she said. "What the hell am I going to say to that whole line of people tomorrow?"

"Tell them the Virgin is still there. You can touch them. They can touch each other."

"They won't believe that."

"They've got to have faith. They have faith."

She kept rubbing. Her hand strayed a little lower.

"Don't fall in love with one of those señoritas," she said.

Oh shit. "Damn it, Julie." Did she have to figure out everything?

PART THREE

SEVENTEEN

The problems began at Dallas-Fort Worth. We'd gotten out of Raleigh a little late, but had an hour to make the connection, and I was never worried. The connection in Mexico City was an hour and a half, so that wasn't a problem either. But in Dallas they first announced that they were having a problem with the computer ("Please do get the fucking computer fixed," the little woman beside me said. "Pardon my French.") and had to get a computer expert into the cockpit. They were harder to find than a normal repairman.

Finally, after about fifty minutes, the computer was okay, but they found someone from the passenger list who was not on the plane. He had checked luggage, so they had to sort through all the bags and get his out.

"Probably a terrorist," my seatmate said.

I hadn't planned to go to Oaxaca. I thought I'd stop in Mexico City to see the Basilica of the Virgin of Guadalupe. But Padre Roberto, when I'd talked to him on that last day, thought I should visit that Virgin last.

"How long will you be in the country?" he said.

"My ticket is open-ended."

"My God. What an opportunity."

He thought I should go see what he called the three Virgins, one in a suburb of Guadalajara, one in Oaxaca City, and the famous one at the Basilica. That would be the crowning experience. Since I already had the ticket to Mexico City, I should connect from there to Oaxaca.

"That won't be hard to schedule. There are flights all day."

There was one that fit right into my itinerary.

"I don't understand why you're going now," Padre Roberto said. "You're doing so well."

I tried to explain how uncomfortable I felt in my situation, all the focus on me, none on what I was teaching.

"It's not that way with the Latinos," he said. "They think it's the Virgin who does the healing. She picked you to help."

"Julie is very welcoming," I said. "She'll take care of them."

"They have faith in you."

"She has magic hands. They'll see. And she understands the Virgin better than I do."

Padre Roberto frowned. I hated to disappoint him.

"I'm worn out," I said. "Need to get away and be alone. Meditate."

"You can do that here."

"There's something I'm trying to understand, that I see in the people I've helped. Juan had it, goofy as he was. Person after person among the Latinos. I don't know what to call it. A way of giving up the self. I want to see where that comes from. Be around it for a while."

"You'll see all kinds of things in Mexico. Machismo. Racism. Huge wealth. Drunkenness and drug problems. It's not perfect."

"I'm not looking for perfect."

"But the thing you're looking for is all over Mexico, in little pockets."

"Blessed are the poor, I keep thinking."

"The poor can be angry, venal, violent, bitter. They have all the vices of the world. But they also are blessed, which is why Jesus hung out with them. They understood."

Padre Roberto knew what I meant.

"There's a guy you should look up in Oaxaca, from our parish. Charles Weymouth. He's showing his parents around, has been there many times. He'll be a great resource."

He gave me the guy's email.

So I was off to Mexico, looking for I knew not what. Mostly just getting away from the situation I'd created.

"I must have the last seat on this godforsaken plane," my seatmate had said as she arrived, a little old woman with a pursed mouth, jutting chin. "That's what comes from last-minute plans. Do you have to sit there?"

"This is my seat."

"Do you have to have the aisle?"

There were two seats on our side. I was happy to take the window.

"There's a shot of tequila in it if you move." She actually winked. "I like to make a quick getaway."

It wouldn't be all that quick. For one thing, we had the last seats on the plane, every single one in front of us taken. For another, the woman moved laboriously. Full of spirit, but the flesh was weak.

"The window seat makes me antsy," she said. "You'll have a great view of Mexico City, coming in. Never seen anything like it."

"You've been there."

"Dozens of times. Coming to celebrate my eightieth birthday."

"You don't look it." Closer to ninety.

"I'm Dolores."

"Hank." I shook her small arthritic hand.

A young woman took the seat in front of us. I would have said girl—she looked seventeen—except that she was carrying a baby. She was blond and pale, with a voluptuous figure. The baby looked as dark as she was light. He looked indigenous.

Where'd she get that baby? were the words that crossed my mind.

"See?" Dolores said. "The men in Mexico are charming. So romantic."

Sounded like the voice of experience.

"Until they get drunk and beat the piss out of you," she said. "That's another story."

A Latin man joined the young woman. "He's the guy?" Dolores said. "So handsome. A little old for her."

Dolores kept up a running commentary. If she hadn't been so entertaining it would have driven me nuts.

Once the crew announced the delay, people could use their cell phones. Immediately half the plane started yacking.

"Kee-rist," Dolores said. "I hate those little phones."

"I finished your manuscript," the guy across the aisle from us said. "I had to call you immediately."

"Especially because my flight was delayed," Dolores said.

"I was ravished by it. Absolutely ravished."

"Oh, Jesus. Pardon my French."

Dolores muttered these things so only I could hear them. I hoped.

The woman in front of us made a call too. "I hope I don't miss the connection to Oh-a-hawk-a City," she was saying.

"Poor thing can't even pronounce it. That can't be her husband."

"I think it's a marvelous achievement," the guy said. "Best student writing I've seen in years."

"And the grand prize is my schlong."

"There's plenty of time," the young woman said. "If we just get off the ground."

"I hope we're over Mexico if we go down," Dolores said.

"You do?" I said.

"That's where I want to die. They know death in that country. Worship it."

"Thank you, Daddy," the young woman said. "I'll call when we land."

"I wonder what Daddy thought when that dark little baby popped out," Dolores said. "Not the grandson of his dreams."

"If you remember one thing from this conversation," the man said. "Remember this."

"I-want-to-dork-you."

"Hacks promote. Artists create."

"Where's the vomit bag?" Dolores rummaged in her pocketbook, pulled out, of all things, a flask. "Our only hope."

"How'd you get that through security?" I said.

"They let you through if it's empty."

"It's not empty now."

"I have a friend in one of the airport bars. My nephew, actually. He's a good kid. Especially since he did time. Paid his debt to society."

Good grief.

"I've never given a moment's thought to promoting my work," the guy said.

"Which is why he's a total unknown," Dolores said. "I promised you a nip." She offered the flask.

"I'll wait."

"I don't normally start this early. But those phones."

"Even if I have to teach freshman comp," the man said. "I never will."

"Never say no to José Cuervo. Where you headed?"

"Oaxaca, first of all. Then Guadalajara. Back to Mexico City. Maybe some places in between. I haven't decided."

"You've been before?"

"Never."

"How much time do you have?"

"Until the money runs out."

"That's the Mexican way. How are you fixed?"

"So-so. I want it to last."

"It will, believe me. You could retire down here."

I could send for Julie.

"You're running from something," she said.

"In a way. Nothing romantic."

"Americans go south when they're on the lam. Like OJ."

"Nothing that bad."

"Think they're safe down there. There's nothing safe about it."

Finally the guy across the aisle finished his call, was chatting up his seatmate, in Spanish no less.

"Do you believe this bird?" she said. "Now he'll nail a Latino woman. How's your espagnol?"

"About halfway."

"Use it. Makes all the difference. It's making a difference for this dingbat. Her pants are wet already."

My Spanish, alas, wasn't good enough to follow.

"Don't mess with Mexican women," Dolores said. "They flirt and don't mean it. Their husbands want to kill you. They do mean it."

"I believe it."

"The men have mistresses. Which is where the hypocrisy comes in. But the whores are beautiful and need money. Buy some condoms."

"I'm past it, to be honest."

"You might find the fountain of youth down here."

That's what Julie was afraid of.

"They hang out in a park near my hotel. Like anybody in Mexico. Trying to make a buck."

"The woman I *am* interested in, the one place I want to go, is the Basilica of the Virgin."

"There's no place in Mexico that shows more about the people. You're Catholic?"

"No. I sometimes go to Mass."

"She doesn't care if you're Muslim. She's your mother. Your true mother."

What a statement.

"The mother of the whores as well. They adore her."

The train of logic was moving right along. I wondered if Dolores was slightly drunk.

"And men are on their knees to both of them. Like Baldy over there."

He was deeply into his conversation with the woman. His Spanish seemed superb.

After a thirty-minute delay they fixed the computer, after another forty they found the bag. By the time we got airborne, I had ten minutes to make my connection.

"Ain't gonna happen," Dolores said. "They'll put you on the next one."

She had me take out my notebook and write things to do. She mentioned a B&B in Oaxaca. "You can go cheaper," she said. "But this place is lovely, and the restaurant's great."

She had another in Guadalajara. "They're a couple of queers, sweet boys. You won't find better hosts anywhere. *Great* Margaritas."

She went on and on about her Mexico City hotel. "Don't run around too much. You learn more staying in one place. And don't see sights. Wander at random. Talk to the bellboys. Sit in the parks. And really, have a whore. Just one. They need the cash. Are you married?"

"I've got a woman."

"She's not who you're running from."

"She's holding down the fort."

"She won't mind. Your one chance to know Mexico deeply. Like plowing the soil."

I do think she was plastered at that point. She told me to get Sprite or ginger ale when they gave us drinks. I don't normally imbibe on planes but what the hell. She gave me quite a hit, didn't stint on herself. She freshened hers later but I passed. "You've got to slow down in Mexico," she said. "They're on a different rhythm."

You didn't have to come to a complete stop.

"But don't forget latex," she said, "when you visit our friends."

We were back to the whores.

"I'll stick with the Virgin," I said.

"You're going to have a major experience with her. She likes it when her children come home."

I did have an odd feeling, entering this alien culture, that I was somehow coming home.

We finally touched down and I had seven minutes to make the connection. Had to pick up luggage and go through customs.

The Latin man in front of us walked off by himself. Apparently he wasn't with the blond. The bald guy walked off with the Latin woman, heading—according to Dolores— for the airport hotel. Dolores waited while the young blond woman gathered her things. She held the baby slung against her, like a peasant woman. Seemed totally comfortable.

"I got a connection to Oh-a-hawk-a City," she said.

"I don't think you'll make it, sweetheart. Hank is going too. But there'll be another. You say, Wuh-*hawk*-a. You've got to get that right."

"Wuh-*hawk*-a," she said. "I knew it was something. My husband talks with all these clicks."

"Where is your husband, baby?"

"Waiting in Oaxaca."

"We'll get you there. Can we help with your things?"

"I got this satchel full of bottles. Milk for Patrick for the next two days."

"What a beautiful name. Is that for his father?"

"It is."

For a brief weird moment I thought the kid was Irish.

"Patricio," Dolores said. "I'm Dolores. And you?"

"Heather."

"We'll take care of you, sweetheart."

I hoped to God Heather didn't think Dolores was my wife.

I was so excited to be in Mexico that for a brief despicable moment I wanted to ditch everybody, let Heather and Dolores stumble out on their own. If Dolores hadn't grabbed the aisle seat, I might have. Leave it to a profane, tequila-swilling whore lover to restore my sense of compassion. We were quite a quartet as we tottered off the plane, Heather with Patricio, who was dead to the world, Dolores, who was drunk, and me, toting a sack of baby bottles. How the hell did I get mixed up in this?

Our progress was agonizing.

"How's your espagnol, darling?" Dolores said.

"Haven't learned that yet."

Shit.

"Wouldn't do me much good. Patricio's family only speaks Indian."

"Indian?" I said to Dolores.

"Some Mixtec dialect. That's what the clicks are about."

This I had to hear.

"How's Patricio's English?" Doris said. "The papa."

"He tries. He's funny."

"This was pure sex," Dolores muttered to me. "Animal magnetism. What a force."

At the top of the ramp was mass confusion, crowds of people hurtling by, others standing around. A representative told us we had to go to 22A, where domestic connections were.

"Do that first," Dolores said. "Before you go through customs. You've got to get a flight."

Heather looked lost. Even I was intimidated.

"Listen, Hank." Dolores took me aside. "You've got some Spanish. She's got none."

"Right."

"This place will eat a girl like that alive. Especially a blond. Stay with her no matter what."

"I will."

"She told me she's got forty dollars. That and a bank card that might not work. You have money?"

"I'm fine."

"I might see you at customs. This is your good deed for the day. Maybe the year." She actually kissed me. "I'm glad you're here."

It was by far the largest airport I'd ever been in, wasn't built for convenience. Gate 22A was about a quarter mile away. Heather and I passed customs, and I was tempted, but kept going.

"I'm slowing you down," Heather said. "I'm sorry."

"It's fine."

All I'd really wanted was to be in Mexico. I was in Mexico.

"I thought Dolores was your mother."

Thank God. "I met her on the plane. What a character.'"

"I'm glad she was there. Don't know what I would have done."

I was more ashamed than ever.

At 22A, they told us the only remaining flight to Oaxaca had been cancelled. We needed to reschedule. They couldn't do that. We had to go back to the airlines.

"I got to call Daddy," Heather said. "He's the only one who can contact Patricio."

He knew the clicking sounds?

We went to Customs and Dolores was nowhere in sight. It wasn't terribly crowded—nearly 6:00—and I got through in a few minutes. Heather was waved to another line and I tried to wait, but somebody made me move along.

Baggage claim was a madhouse. Dolores had her bags.

"I told you not to leave Heather!"

"She got moved to another line. She'll be through."

"Those people are going to wonder about that baby."

But in a few minutes she showed up. I hadn't found my bags. She couldn't find hers either.

The guys at baggage claim didn't speak English. Dolores was fluent—I should have guessed—and seemed to give them hell. They told her the bags must have gone to Oaxaca, but she said they couldn't have. There wasn't time. We needed to check with Mexicana, the guy said.

"That's all the clothes I got," Heather said. "I hope they didn't lose those bags."

Forty dollars to her name.

"Keep looking, sweetheart. They might come. Let me talk to Hank."

Heather looked forlorn. "Daddy said I shouldn't come. But Patricio hasn't seen his baby."

"You were right, sweetheart. Love conquers all."

We'd see if it could conquer the Mexican baggage system.

Dolores took me aside. "This is some weird situation. I'm an old lady with a pint of tequila in me and can't help. I'm sorry."

"I've got it covered."

I was a little woozy myself. Hadn't eaten for hours.

"I'm giving you two hundred dollars. Give it to her when I'm gone."

"That's sweet."

"Don't flash the money. Give it to her in a safe place." She slipped it into my hands. "There's something about that baby. He hasn't cried once."

I'd noticed.

"That's Mary and the baby Jesus, I swear. You can't leave them alone."

"I won't."

"Once you're out of security you're in a snake pit. Don't take anybody's help. Don't speak to anybody who says taxi. Don't, for God's sake, ask for help from a cop. Just talk to airline people."

"All right."

"I'm at the Maria Cristina. If you need to stay somewhere come there. I'll pay."

"We'll be fine."

The airport was nicer once we got out of security. The wing we were in was new. It was true that every third person said, "Taxi?" Some followed up with "Informacion?" Patricio finally started to stir, though he wasn't crying, but Heather said he needed to eat. We found a place for her to sit outside some restrooms, and I went to deal with the airlines.

It would be hard to exaggerate the distances I walked. I tried several Mexicana desks. No one knew the first thing about luggage. They said that if it hadn't gone to Oaxaca it might be waiting for the next flight, in the morning. They couldn't help me with scheduling. I'd have to take that up with American.

At that point I was starving. I went to the place where I'd left Heather but she wasn't there. At least I thought it was the place. I walked a ways further, found more restrooms, but she wasn't there either. I started to ask people if they'd seen a blond girl with a Mexican baby but no one had. I got frantic, ran from one bathroom to another. Finally she stepped out of the first one.

"My cell phone don't work," she said. "I don't get what's wrong."

"Do you have international coverage?"

"I don't know. My Daddy got it."

She tried my cell, called her father, told him the situation. "There's this man helping me. An American. An older gentleman. It's fine, Daddy."

He's at least eighty.

We walked the immense distance to the American counter. I thought of stopping to eat—we passed restaurants—but ticket counters were closing down. The American counter was dark except for one agent. She was taking care of a family when I arrived. That took ten minutes. The one guy in front of me in line was buying a ticket, and that took another fifteen. She wrote it up by hand. He paid cash, and she didn't have change, had to go off and find it. We'd been standing there for thirty-five minutes when we got to the front. She was going to help me or I was going to kill her.

"I missed a flight to Oaxaca tonight. I was on the American flight from Dallas."

"You must be Señor Wilder," she said. "Did you go off and take a tour of the city?"

"I feel like I did. On foot."

"I have your ticket for a morning flight to Oaxaca."

I couldn't believe it. After this endless wait—people paid for airline tickets *with cash* and the clerk had to go off and *get change?*—she knew my name.

She also spoke excellent English.

"I've been waiting for you," she said.

"I was trying to get a flight to Oaxaca."

"I'm very sorry. There's not another until morning. But you're booked on that. We also have you booked for a night in the airport Camino Real. And vouchers for three meals."

"Three?"

"It's our policy. Though you might not want three before seven in the morning, when your flight is."

I'd do my damnedest.

I nodded toward Heather. "She's in the same situation."

"This is Señora ... Melendez?" She frowned just slightly. *Could that be possible*, she seemed to be saying.

"Yes," Heather said. I hadn't known her last name. It was a shocker.

"And that is"—now she really did frown—"Patrick?"

Right. The little Irishman.

"What about our luggage?" I said.

"It's safe, but it was transferred to Mexicana for the morning flight. I know that's inconvenient. I'm sorry."

I'd be eating all night anyway.

"But since you have no luggage you can check in at Mexicana now. Then you can arrive just a half hour early in the morning."

I smiled. "We've been chasing all over the airport."

"I'm sorry, Señor. You should have come here first."

I simultaneously felt like an idiot and experienced a tremendous sense of relief.

The first thing we did, just outside the gate in a little food court, was call Heather's father, on my phone. After a few minutes he wanted to talk to me. I could tell that was coming when she said, "It's okay, Daddy. He's *old*."

"I don't know who you are, mister," he said on the phone.

"I'm a high school teacher from North Carolina." That sounded better than a Zen teacher, who would most certainly have fucked his daughter. "Down here for the first time. Missed the same flight Heather did."

"How's your Spanish?" He pronounced it *Spainish*.

"Better than hers."

"That wouldn't be hard. This is a friggin' mess. I told her not to go down there."

"Everything's fine. We've got a hotel for the night. Flight in the morning."

"I've heard about them Mexi hotels."

"This is a four-star hotel. Camino Real. You can look it up on the Internet." I'd looked it up when I researched Oaxaca. Way out of my range.

"Where the hell am I going to get Internet at this hour?"

Hmm. "Anyway, it'll be fine."

"I'm sorry, mister. I'm a nervous wreck. She's just out of school herself. You could've taught her."

"I figured."

"Maybe you got kids."

"One son. He's thirty-four." *He* would like to fuck her.

"I'd appreciate you looking after her. Stay with her until she's with Patricio, if you would. He's a tough hombre. Everything'll be fine."

"I'll do that."

Heather talked to him again. He said he'd get international service on her phone. Hadn't known they needed that. He'd get word to Patricio.

How, he didn't say. It sure as hell wouldn't be the Internet.

The whole place suddenly looked different. I would have suggested a snack except for the vast amounts of free food at the hotel. We walked the quarter mile to Mexicana but it seemed like a stroll in the moonlight. I didn't care how many guys said *taxi*. We checked in at Mexicana for the next morning, and by some miracle the hotel was right across the way. I expected a half-mile walk.

As we walked across the ramp, I said, "This is going to be the nicest hotel you've ever seen."

"I haven't seen that many."

I figured the Camino Real could match anything in Pensacola.

We stepped into a little corridor and I stopped Heather there.

"Dolores gave me some money for you, a little cushion," I said. "She wanted you to have it."

"Oh God." She looked as if I'd pulled a gun. "What is it?"

"Two hundred dollars. You don't need it now. But it'll let you relax."

Right at the moment, it made her extremely tense.

"Daddy asked if you gave me any money."

"This is from Dolores. There's no way we can give it back."

The hotel was a modern stone building, built on the Mexican courtyard design, though the courtyard was enclosed by a roof, rooms all around. The lighting was oddly dim. There was a large restaurant at the front, café and bar in the back. The folks at the desk took our vouchers and showed us up. I had the standard hotel room: two doubles, cable TV, a gleaming new bathroom. A huge window looked on the airport, which was a majestic structure when you weren't walking for miles inside it. I watched planes come down. It was mesmerizing.

I was so hungry at that point that I felt full.

It was almost eight o'clock when I got downstairs. Predictably, the voucher was for the café, not the restaurant. Also, predictably, it didn't include alcohol. The waiter told me that with a deep sadness in his eyes.

"*It doesn't matter,*" I said. "*I have money.*" He brightened considerably. "Negra Modelo, por favor."

He brought me some spicy peanuts with the beer. I fell on them like a starving man.

That first beer lasted all of about ninety seconds.

"*I'm sorry, señor,*" I said, in my best Spanish. "*I had a difficult day.*"

"*Another beer,*" he said, beaming.

I liked his attitude. He brought another dish of peanuts as well.

By the time Heather came down I was halfway through the peanuts and three-quarters finished with my beer. I figured she would think they were my first.

Neither of us had freshened up because there was nothing to freshen with. Patricio was the one person who had weathered the trip without a hitch. He still hadn't cried.

"The voucher doesn't include alcohol," I said, "but I'd be happy to buy you a drink."

"Daddy said not to let you."

"We won't tell him."

"I heard a Margarita is good."

As she said that, two questions went through my mind. First: is she old enough to drink? Next: does anyone in Mexico care?

The waiter took her order without a blink.

When her drink arrived she took a sip, leaned back, and—without my asking—told me the most romantic story I'd ever heard in my life.

She'd met Patricio the summer before, when she'd graduated from high school and was working at a root beer stand. There was a construction site nearby, and the workers came over for lunch.

"The American guys was disgusting. All red and sunburnt and dirty, fat from the beer they drink at night, full of dumb remarks. Saying awful things to me. The Mexicans was shy and polite. Never said nothing."

Probably because they couldn't.

"There was one who was *so* good looking. Like Elvis when he started out, with that long slick hair. Real thin. But way darker."

Elvis wasn't exactly a blond.

"I could tell he liked me, just by the way he looked. But he never said a thing."

It was a pretty good guess that any young man liked Heather, especially a Latin. She was luscious.

"Then he started coming by alone in the evening. For supper."

We were interrupted to order. I was glad Heather hadn't thrown down the Margarita like lemonade. She'd been staring at the menu since she arrived, all through our conversation, finally said, "I'm going to get something exotic." *Menudo, pozole,* I was thinking. "A ribeye steak and baked potato," she said, completely serious. I guess they didn't serve those at the root-beer stand. The waiter said that exceeded her allotment, but he spoke Spanish, so I told him to put the excess with the drinks. It turned out the airline was chintzy after all.

I had no idea what the man thought of us as a couple. With our little child.

I was rather full at that point, what with all the peanuts. I ordered enchiladas and another beer (no surprise to the waiter). I wasn't having a ribeye my first night in Mexico.

This was just a café, but I wasn't disappointed by the waiters. They took our orders as if we were discriminating gourmets, carried the trays with a flare, made serving even a beer and peanuts into a little ceremony. I was to notice that all over Mexico.

"So he came around in the evening," I said.

"And walked me home," she said. "I live close by."

"But he didn't speak English."

"A lot more than I speak *Spainish*. He was just so sweet. I could tell. Pretty soon we wanted to get married." That was quick. "But we couldn't, because he was illegal." A slight technicality. "Then I found out I was pregnant."

What followed was so complicated and devious that I had no idea how they figured it out, this Mexican construction worker and voluptuous clerk at a root-beer stand who could barely communicate. Patricio could return to Mexico and apply for a visa to be with his wife and child, but not if he'd been in this country illegally. He had to hide the fact that he'd been there.

He returned to Mexico. They apparently don't hunt you down when you're going back. Heather followed. They "fell in love" there—very quickly—and got married, in time to make the pregnancy look legitimate. She returned to the States, kept in touch with her husband, had her baby. He applied for permission to join the wife whom he'd "met" in Mexico, and the child who'd been conceived there. It was a long process, but his chances looked good. In the meantime, she was visiting to show him and her in-laws the new child.

"He's meeting you at the airport."

"We were supposed to be on a bus tonight to his house. It's another eight hours there. We figured the baby would do best at night, when he was asleep."

What an ordeal. Patricio must live way off somewhere.

"I hope he isn't too worried," she said. "I hope he'll wait."

"He'll wait. Are you kidding?"

Our exotic meal had long since come. I was amazed that Heather could eat it, and carry on that conversation, while holding Patricio in her left arm. It was as if he were melded to her.

We shared a flan for dessert. Dolores told me to have flan everywhere.

We went to the gift shop to buy toiletries. I bought a t-shirt to sleep in, and Heather brought an extra-large one. It wasn't going to be a terribly long night anyway. I was exhausted.

As we got into the elevator, she said, "I'm a little scared."

"The hotel is safe," I said. "It isn't that long until we fly to Oaxaca."

"I never been alone in a place like this. All these Mexicans around."

She'd better get used to that.

There did seem to be an unusual number of men hanging around in the lobby. I didn't know if they worked at the place or what.

"Please don't take this the wrong way, but my room's got two nice big beds. Would you mind sleeping in one of them?"

Only if you'll leave off the t-shirt.

"I don't know, Heather. I snore. At least people tell me I do." Julie went on and on about it.

"Patricio does too." I looked at the kid. Didn't seem possible. "I mean his papa. I don't mind. I'd feel better if you was there."

"Yes."

"Don't tell Daddy, of course. He said you'd be trying to get in."

How the hell would I tell Daddy? Though we seemed to call him every five minutes.

I could see her point. She was a young woman—and that was being generous—with an infant a few months old. It was a strange place, and she found it intimidating. I, on the other hand, longed to be alone for a few hours. I was ready to crash.

It wasn't going to happen.

I stopped at my room to get my carry-on, which held just a couple of books and my meditation cushion. Heather's room was exactly like mine except everything faced in the other direction. Patricio had started to stir so she said she'd feed him. I went to the bathroom to get ready.

I hadn't considered the situation. All I had was my boxers—all I slept in anyway—and my new t-shirt. I brushed and flossed, took a long shower with all the shampoos and lotions. It felt great. I thought of putting my pants back on but that seemed ridiculous. I would just be taking them off. I walked out in my boxers. I felt like a young bride.

Heather was changing Patricio. "Your cell phone rang," she said. "I thought I'd better not answer."

Thank God. "It was probably my girlfriend."

"I thought you was married. Having a son and all."

"Divorced. A long time ago. This woman is something new."

And she was convinced that the first thing I'd do in Mexico was find some young girl.

Her message was brief. "Hank, you said you were going to call when you got in and I haven't heard a word. I'm sure everything's fine, but please call and leave a message on my cell so I won't worry all day tomorrow. I'm going to bed."

She sounded fine. Slightly annoyed.

"Is Patricio out for the night?" I said.

"Looks like it."

All I needed was a baby wailing in the background.

Julie picked up when I called, though she said she wouldn't. Sounded half asleep.

"I made it to Mexico, but not to Oaxaca," I said. I'd given up all pretense of hiding that from her. She'd guessed half of it. "The flight was late and there were no more connections. It's been a long day. I meant to call but didn't have a chance."

"I figured it was something."

"I was in the shower when you called." The scrumptious blond didn't want to pick up.

"Everybody was clamoring for El Señor this morning."

"I'm sure you did fine."

"I touched people. Nothing happened."

"That's the way I feel. It happens at some other level."

Or doesn't. Who knows?

"They were not happy."

"Tell them healing is everywhere. Faith is everywhere."

Patricio sneezed, quite moistly.

"Bless you," Julie said.

"Thanks."

"I found out prostitution is legal in many Mexican states. The girls are beautiful. Although there are some real old ones for guys who don't have much money."

"They're probably about my age."

This was sounding like Julie from twenty years ago.

Patricio sneezed again.

"You're not catching cold, are you?"

"It's just the air conditioning."

"Call me when you get there. Keep me in the loop."

"There is no loop. But I'll call."

No sooner had I hung up than Patricio farted. "Goodness," Heather said.

Glad I hadn't had to explain that. The frijoles down here are really rough.

Heather left Patricio on the bed, went in to take a bath.

I thought I should call Dolores, found the number of the Maria Cristina and made the call. It wasn't until the phone was ringing that I realized—this was really stupid—that I didn't know her last name.

The sentence that I muttered over the phone would be roughly translated, "*There is an old woman from the United States named Dolores.*"

"*Yes,* señor," the guy said. "*One moment.*"

They probably got calls like that all the time.

"Hank," she said. "I'm a little tanked up at the moment."

What a shock.

I filled her in on everything, told her we'd be getting a 7:00 flight.

"Somehow or other I'm spending the night in her room," I said. "She was nervous."

"And you got a hard-on like a chorizo."

Dolores had had a few.

"I think that's good," she said. "She needs somebody there. But no funny stuff, big boy."

"Really, Dolores."

"Her husband probably carries a razor. He'll know when he meets you if you did something. They got an instinct."

Wonderful.

"The more I think about this, the stranger it gets," she said. "These indigenous people off in the hills."

"Eight hours from Oaxaca City by bus."

"Tonight she's in the Camino Real, tomorrow night she'll have a dirt floor. No running water. Make Pensacola look like Park Avenue."

I hadn't pictured that.

"She's going to get sick. The baby's going to get sick. Hell, you'll probably get sick. And when this finally gets resolved, if it does get resolved, which is no sure thing, he'll work construction in the States. *If* things go well. She'll work retail. They'll have five or six kids. What kind of life will that be?"

Sounded grim.

"All the same, that's a special child. And a sweet, innocent mother, even if she did sneak off and dork some Mexican guy. There's something about them. I can feel it."

I didn't know whether that was deep spiritual intuition or tequila. I looked over at Patricio. He was staring at the ceiling, boogying.

"So you take care of them, Hank. Get that baby back to his father. I'd help if I could."

But she was drowning in a sea of tequila.

After I hung up I went over to Patricio for a while. Talk about enlightened. Babies are at one with everything. The energy just flows. You can see it.

Zazen is about recovering all that. I don't know how far back we have to go.

I put my hand on his chest. Pure energy. What a miracle.

By the time Heather came out I was lying under the covers. I can't fully describe the effect of that t-shirt. Thank God it was an extra large. She was a throwback to the fifties glamour girls, big breasts, big bottom, maybe a little extra around the middle but who cares. Her hair was blond and hung over her shoulders, her complexion pure peaches and cream.

Somehow her figure, which hadn't shown up in her airport clothes, did make an appearance in that t-shirt. Everything wobbled and jiggled. She wasn't in the least self-conscious.

"Want me to wash your underwear?" she said.

"My underwear?"

"I'm washing mine. You feel better in the morning with clean pants. They'll dry out if I hang them up."

She wasn't wearing underpants. As I had that thought, my eyes instinctively looked down, and sure enough, I saw a little shadow.

The t-shirt had about an inch to spare.

"You can throw them to me," she said.

"I might have to get up in the night. I definitely will." Have you heard of the prostate?

"We'll have the lights off. You can get up first. It's no big deal."

It wasn't every day a woman offered to wash your underpants.

"All right. What the hell. I appreciate it."

I took them off and tossed them to her.

"No problem."

She went to the sink and washed our underpants. To do that, she leaned forward slightly. It isn't that I was staring, at least I hope not. That t-shirt did creep up.

I'd honestly thought what Dolores said was ridiculous. I hadn't given, would not give a thought to touching Heather. She was half the age of my son. But I hadn't imagined this. My throat went dry, and I felt myself swallow.

They say that a sixty-year-old man—I was fifty-nine, but let's not quibble—no longer gets spontaneous erections. It takes a great deal of direct stimulation to get him up. I've found that to be true. There are exceptions.

Old Dolores. She was a prophet.

Heather hung up the underpants and got into her bed.

"Hope I don't snore too much," I said. At this rate I wouldn't sleep at all.

"It'll be fine. I just appreciate you. Patricio does too."

I felt sure she meant the little guy.

"I just hope they have my luggage in the morning," she said. "There's stuff in there I can't replace."

The same thing worried me. Everything they'd said about the luggage sounded weird.

"There's one strange thing about me I should mention," I said.

"You're a compulsive masturbator. It's okay."

I blushed.

"That's a joke we used to make at church camp," she said.

I laughed. Those Pentecostal church camps. "No. I practice zazen in the morning. Sitting meditation."

"Will I have to get out?"

"I just get up and sit on a cushion and stare at the wall. It's a religious practice."

"It won't hurt Patricio?"

"Won't hurt anybody. I'm just sitting there. I might not do it tomorrow, since we're getting up early. But if I wake up early, I will. You can move around, get dressed, anything you want. You won't disturb me."

"All right."

"I just didn't want to freak you out."

I didn't need to worry about sleeping. Hard-on or not, voluptuous young woman or not: In the old days that might have kept me awake half the night or made me do some awkward thing I'd regret forever, but excitement at my age was just a pleasant buzz. The idea of touching a beautiful young woman like Heather was absurd.

I was also exhausted and carrying three beers. I did have a powerful erotic dream. Patricio cried around 3:00, and Heather fed him. And true to the internal clock that never fails me, I woke up before 5:00, stumbled half naked into the bathroom (the wrong half) and found my underpants, which were—thank God—dry. I sat for thirty-five minutes before the hotel's call came through.

Heather never ate breakfast, said she'd meet me in the lobby. Breakfast is my favorite meal, and huevos rancheros are better in Mexico than anyplace I've been in the States. I'd just finished when Heather came down.

The airport was empty. No one asked if I wanted a taxi. The Mexicana counter was close but we had to walk a considerable distance to security, much further to the gate. The airport shops were starting to open, the sky to our right—out where the planes were—still dark. Heather got a Coke at a shop near our gate, which was all she ever had in the morning. A true Southern girl. She used to have a cigarette with it but was trying to stop for Patricio (the little guy), had some Nicorette gum.

Patricio was his usual placid self. She gave him a bottle.

"That stuff you were doing this morning, was that Hindu?"

"Buddhist. Zen Buddhist."

"Is it praying?"

"It's like praying, but you don't say anything."

Heather hadn't studied comparative religions at Pensacola High School.

"How does that work?"

"You let God do the talking. Except he doesn't talk. Hard to explain."

"Because I was going to say, if you want to pray for something, pray our luggage is on that airplane."

Even God could not fathom the Mexican baggage system.

"Daddy thinks that stuff is Satanic. Hindu and Buddha and all that."

That Hindu was quite a guy.

"We better not tell him." Since I wasn't in your room anyway.

"He also thinks Catholics are from Satan. That Virgin Mary stuff. Patricio's Catholic."

"What do you think?"

"Patricio says it's Mary who got him across the border, so I got to be thankful for that."

"What does your father think of Patricio?"

"He was mad at first. Wanted to kill him. For real." Totally matter of fact as she said that. "But the construction guy told him Patricio was one of his best. Worked all day without stopping. Sent his money home. Didn't drink beer with the others.

Though that wasn't completely true. But he don't get plastered every night. Loves his mama, all his brothers and sisters. I knew he was sweet the first time I met him."

On that basis, she had his child.

"His mama is four feet high, I swear. Little bitty thing. Doesn't even speak Spainish. Just clicks and clicks. But she loves me to death. Keeps on hugging me."

I noticed a few people who had been on the flight from Dallas. They were the ones with the old, wrinkled clothes. Before long—right on time—we were called for our flight. Heather was up front; I was way in the back. She said she'd wait for me when we got off.

The flight was uneventful, though beautiful in the morning sky. Our snack was cookies. One Mexican guy had a Tecate. 7:15 a.m.

The Oaxaca airport was tiny. I wasn't expecting Mexico City, but this was smaller than Raleigh, circa 1966. And it was international. The baggage claim area was a single track, maybe twenty feet long, people jammed into a small space all around it. Even if I'd seen my bag I wouldn't have been able to get it. A number of the bags were going unclaimed.

There were two areas of high tension. One was the baggage area, where people were straining to see their bags, hoping to see them, crossing themselves. The other was a waiting area outside, where a large crowd waited to see who had arrived. They were four or five deep. But if we left the luggage area, we couldn't come back. We couldn't go out without our bags.

"I don't see Patricio," Heather said. She kept edging to that side of the room.

"He's probably there. It's such a crowd."

"He'd be right at the front. He'd kill to be at the front. Looking for me."

"He's here somewhere. We just need to get our bags."

Which may itself have been impossible.

Two things puzzled me. One was that many Mexicans had immense amounts of luggage. A family of three might have nine or ten pieces. Some were enormous ancient suitcases; others were mammoth cardboard boxes all taped up. They seemed to have whole rolls of tape on them, bulging and misshapen, impossible to carry. There people were, struggling with them.

The other was that we seemed to be going through customs, when we already had. Our bags hadn't, it was true—those of us from the Dallas flight—but we were only a small number. Besides, how would anyone have known?

I tried to ask one guy the customs questions but we got engaged in a weird Who's-on-First-type Spanish conversation. Why do we have to go through customs? Because it is required of all passengers. But this flight is from Mexico City. To be sure, señor, the flight is from Mexico City. Isn't that a domestic flight? Of course, a flight from Mexico City is domestic. Then why do we have to go through customs? Because all passengers are required to.

He seemed happy to have that conversation all day long. His function was to stand there and drive gringos out of their minds.

It was encouraging that some people from our flight actually got their bags. One Mexican family after another got their massive amount of luggage and proceeded to the adjoining space, also rather small, to go through customs. What was discouraging was that you couldn't go through without your luggage, and you couldn't get in line without it. Everything depended on luggage. Also, the customs line moved at an agonizing pace.

Another discouraging fact was that all the people getting their luggage seemed to be Mexican. The people who stood around empty handed, looking terribly forlorn (also quite pale) were gringos.

You had to push a large button beside a traffic light to get through customs. (Maybe this is true the world over. I haven't traveled much.) If the light was green, you could walk through. If it was red, you had to open your bags. I dearly hoped that was a random process. One Mexican family with eight pieces, including three gargantuan cardboard boxes, came up red. The customs officer took out a knife and sliced into the first box.

Good God.

"I still don't see Patricio," Heather said.

"I know he's out there. Dying to see you."

Eventually—we had been there an hour—the discouraging fact was that the only people without their bags were from the Dallas flight. Three of them had been in the café that morning at breakfast. I checked with the other two. Seven in all.

"I was afraid of this," one of the women said.

"Me too," I said.

I went over to the enigmatic baggage guy, asked if there was any luggage around that had come in the night before. He nodded toward a huge stack of bags in the adjacent room. I walked over to take a look, didn't see my bag among them. I told Heather to check and she couldn't find hers either. When she was over there, she'd had a good look at the people still waiting.

"Patricio isn't out there," she said. She looked ready to cry.

"He's around," I said. "We're going to find him."

I put my arm around her. Some tears popped out and rolled down her face.

"What an adorable baby," one of the women said. "You must be so proud." Her way of speaking carried an unasked question.

"I am," Heather said.

"He's such a beautiful color," the woman said.

"Yes," Heather said.

"Could I hold him?" the woman said.

"No," Heather said.

Any other questions?

After an hour and twenty minutes, a luggage truck came roaring up. Bags started to show up on the track. "That's mine," Heather said.

All our bags were there.

The baggage guy was utterly deadpan. He'd never had any doubt.

Heather was holding Patricio, so I helped with her bags, which were quite large. I had three bags to take care of, so we were the last to go through. There was some confusion that we were one family, but we straightened that out, handed in our custom forms. We both got the green light. When we got out to the outside room, no one was waiting.

"Taxi?" somebody said to me.

Heather leaned against me and burst into tears.

EIGHTEEN

Dolores may have been an old lush, but everything she told me was right on the money. She said that under no circumstances, at any airport in Mexico, should I ever take anything but an official taxi, with a ticket from a taxi stand. She also said that all I had to tell them in Oaxaca was "Casa de las Bugambilias." They'd take care of the rest.

The taxis were large vans meant to take passengers to a number of hotels, but by the time Heather was through bawling we had one to ourselves. Everyone else was gone.

"I don't think I should leave," she said. "How's he ever going to find me? This is where we said we'd meet."

I agreed in theory. And I did not, at that very moment, have a good idea about hooking up with Patricio. I didn't have a clue.

But I was exhausted. I'd spent enough time in that airport for the rest of my life, and there were only hard chairs out in the waiting room, crowded with people and luggage, bathed in dusty sunlight. I couldn't imagine waiting there.

The men around us—guys standing at the taxi stand—were deeply sympathetic. A couple were practically crying themselves. They didn't know what the drama was for this beautiful blond woman and her surprisingly dark baby, but they wanted to help.

One man in particular, a sad-eyed cadaverous guy named Juan Enrique, dressed in an airport uniform. His job was to stand in that waiting room and make sure no one made a sudden dash for the room where people went through customs. Mexicans could be emotional when their loved ones returned.

He was at his post from 7:00 in the morning until 7:00 in the evening. At that time another man took over. For meals, he bought something from vendors in the airport. He never strayed far.

One of the things I grew obsessed with in Mexico was how many people had days like that. Your job is to stand here in uniform all day, looking sad and bored.

I told him our situation. This beautiful young woman was supposed to meet her Mexican husband the evening before, but we had arrived twelve hours late. We had no idea where he might have gone. We'd had an extremely difficult two days, needed to get settled somewhere.

"*Of course you do,*" he said.

The husband's name was Patricio. He was thin and dark, had long slick hair, was extremely good looking.

"*He must have been,*" Juan Enrique said, "*to have found such a beautiful wife.*"

If Patricio came here looking for his wife, Juan Enrique could call me on my cell phone at any time. He himself did not have a cell phone but had access to one. The men at the taxi stand nodded their assent. Whatever expenses people incurred, I would pay those, along with a handsome reward. We would be deeply grateful for their help.

"*Many Mexican men would be happy to act as father to this baby,*" Juan Enrique said. The guys at the taxi stand nodded.

"*We're only looking for the real father,*" I said. "*This young man named Patricio. Please call only for him.*"

The drivers asked who would get the reward if someone else found Patricio. I said that whoever found him would get the reward. One of them gave me his card, in case I wanted to check in. He explained that he was much better equipped than Juan Enrique to look for Patricio.

I persuaded Heather that this was the best alternative. These men would be on the lookout.

The taxi guy assured us that if Patricio existed anywhere in Oaxaca, they would find him.

On the cab ride into town, I clarified a few things. I'd had the impression the evening before that Heather's father had been passing information on to the young man. It turned out he was calling Mexicana, asking them to get word to him. Having seen the way the airport functioned, I wasn't hopeful.

All Patricio really knew was that Heather hadn't been on the plane. Mexicans—according to Dolores—often saw events as a matter of fate. They didn't expect things to go well. They were used to being defeated by circumstances.

"How do you communicate with him most of the time?" I said.

"I call the one phone in the village. Somebody runs off and gets him. It's expensive, but we never talk long. Also, it's hard to get things across on the phone. We do better face to face."

As the presence of young Patricio suggested.

"You're sure he knew what date you were coming."

"We went over it in English and Spainish. I know the days and numbers."

"Would this be a good time to call?"

"Mornings are good, usually."

"Do you have the number?"

"I didn't think I'd need it. Daddy has it."

I wasn't sure I wanted to go through that ordeal.

In the meantime, we entered the heart of Oaxaca. What I noticed—Julie had mentioned this—were the colors. Buildings were adobe and one story, often-run-down, but people didn't limit themselves to the drab colors we did. Bold bright colors and pastels were all over town. It was a feast for the eyes.

I was slightly surprised when we got to the Casa. The street seemed so narrow, but once we got past the street-front restaurant the courtyard was spacious. As soon as I mentioned Dolores, the staff was effusive. A couple spoke excellent English.

I thought I'd have to pay for two rooms, but they had a two-bedroom suite. I explained the situation, that we hoped Heather would be leaving soon, then I'd want a smaller room. I'd take the suite for a day.

We made the obligatory call to her father. He asked to speak to me.

"I'm beside myself, mister, I'll tell you. I'm on the verge of getting her on a plane and bringing her right back."

"I understand."

"Except that I don't know how I'd pay, the penalties and all. Jesus Christ."

It was just as well he couldn't afford it.

"What I can't get, pardon me saying this, you been good to my girl from everything she said, but what I don't get is why you're doing this. You can see why I'd be suspicious, good looking as she is."

"Definitely."

"I been beating guys off with a stick since she was twelve. Know'd all along it would end this way, some little baby and a father we couldn't find. But in Mexico. Jesus Christ."

"I'm helping because she needs it. I speak Spanish and she doesn't."

"You got that right. Much as I been getting after her about it."

"And some old lady on the plane told me this was Mary and the baby Jesus. Made me swear I'd take care of them."

"It ain't the Virgin Mary, that's for sure. And this sure as hell ain't Christmas."

"The woman's been right about everything."

"And Joseph, in this case, is one tough motherfucker, though he don't look it. He'll take care of her if he can just get aholt of her."

"He'll get ahold of her. We'll find him." Half the taxi drivers in Oaxaca were on his trail.

"I appreciate this, mister. It's a hell of a thing, having a daughter."

We tried the number in Patricio's village. An old woman answered, sent a kid off looking. He returned and said that Patricio was with his wife in Oaxaca City. I asked if anyone had heard from him and she said no. I realized how moronic a question that was. I told him her we might be calling the next day, if that wasn't a problem. She said we could call anytime.

I tried to call Dolores, but she wasn't in.

Heather looked dismal.

"We're going to find him," I said. "I'm absolutely sure."

"He might've went home. Might be on his way."

"He wouldn't do that."

"We never talked about this."

I would have thought he'd stay at the airport.

"I can't pay for this," she said. "Once I go through Dolores's money, I'm gone."

"Keep Dolores's money. I've hardly paid anything I wouldn't have anyway."

"But the food and all. I wasn't expecting this."

"I can take care of it. He's going to show up."

I had a feeling.

In the meantime—though there was no saying this to Heather—we weren't exactly in hell. Our suite wasn't

gigantic—just two bedrooms and a bath—but beautifully furnished, quite comfortable. The place smelled wonderful, flowers and soaps and lotions everywhere.

The restaurant was also marvelous. In days to come I would
discover Oaxacan cuisine—a distinct subset of Mexican—but
didn't find a place that served it better than La Olla. For lunch
I had my first Mexican Margarita—considerably better than
its gringo counterpart—and *enchiladas en mole*, which were
extraordinarily rich. Heather had *carne asada* but just picked at
it. She didn't want to drink. Patricio didn't approve.

I tried to take a siesta after lunch but got restless. The way I
explore a new city is by walking. Don't care where I wind up. I
just want the feel of the place.

I knocked on Heather's door and told her I would take a
stroll. She said she'd stay put.

Over time, Oaxaca would become one of my favorite cities for walking, but I preferred the mornings and evenings,
when the shadows were longer. The midday sun is bright and
blinding and dizzying. I was hanging close to the small shadows of buildings.

In one direction—the hostess had mentioned—was a beautiful shady park, a city block around. The other direction was
more touristy, with cobblestone streets, cute little shops, art
galleries, restaurants. At the center of the neighborhood was
a huge church, the Cathedral of Santo Domingo. I couldn't
remember if that was the name Padre Roberto had mentioned,
but I thought I'd have a look. The sun was beating down, and I
felt like getting inside.

I stumbled into one of the great architectural marvels in all
of Mexico, a towering baroque church with elaborately gilded
stucco, especially noticeable when the sun poured through the
stain glass windows, as it did then. I could have spent hours

walking around, taking in details of the walls and ceilings, looking at side chapels. As in nearly all churches in Mexico, there was a beautiful image of the Virgin.

Somehow, nevertheless, the place left me cold. About half of the people were tourists, and though there were multiple notices about not taking pictures, every now and then a flash went off. Mass was taking place, but the building was so vast that—though I sat in a pew—it seemed to be happening way down at the front, didn't carry to where I was.

Some nuns happened in right in front of me, tried to liven things up by singing the hymns loudly, chanting during the Eucharist, but it wasn't much use. People in the pews gazed around. Far down at the front, the priest spoke.

One of the nuns carried a cell phone. Direct line to the Big Guy upstairs, no doubt.

I stayed until the end of Mass out of respect, watched the procession to the back. I walked toward the back myself, turned to look one last time. As I did, I noticed a gringo walking toward me, nicely and casually dressed, in perhaps his mid-fifties. He was gazing toward the floor, tears pouring from his eyes. He had obviously been moved more than I was. When he got to the back he looked up at me and started.

"I just saw you on YouTube," he said.

I smiled. "No." Good grief. Would this never end? "I'm not on YouTube."

"You are. You're Hank Wilder. I watched it before I came over here." He started pulling himself together, wiping his tears, blowing his nose.

"I don't think so." And would you please keep your voice down.

"Father Roberto told me about you this morning. He said you were coming down here. And then I watched it on

YouTube. The Miracle Birth. He told me I should look you up. It's a miracle I ran into you."

"I don't know about that. Catholic Mass, a Sunday."

"But you're Hank Wilder, from down in Durham. You do faith healing. I don't believe you just showed up."

The temptation to deny my name, deny everything I'd done, was overwhelming. This might seem like a miracle to him, but to me it was the worst stroke of luck imaginable.

"That all got out of hand in Durham," I said. "I came to Mexico to get away from it. I hope you'll respect that."

"Of course. But this is the answer to a prayer. Let me tell you."

He said his name was Charles Weymouth, and I remembered Padre Roberto had mentioned him. He'd been visiting Oaxaca, all of Mexico, for many years. He had an enormous personal art collection, mostly Latin art, had found Oaxaca to be a center for that, especially painting. He came almost every year.

For years he'd wanted to bring his parents along, both of whom were now in their eighties. They liked the art but never wanted to come. Finally this year he'd persuaded them, by showing them the website of the Camino Real in Oaxaca. They could have a luxury vacation, spend lots of time by the pool, but also visit the best galleries, which were close by. They would love it.

But on the second day his father was there, five days ago, he'd had a massive stroke. Weymouth's mother had found him lying on the floor. They'd rushed him to a private hospital and got him on a respirator but hadn't been able to get him a vital drug because they didn't know when the stroke happened. Doctors had monitored him ever since. Weymouth was convinced he'd gotten decent care.

There had been some hope for improvement when the swelling went down, so they waited a few days, but things hadn't changed. The best medical opinion from all the doctors was that there was no reason to leave him on the respirator, which was keeping him alive. They were sorry, but his thinking and speaking centers had been destroyed. He couldn't survive as anything more than a vegetable.

That was the fifth day, past which there could be no improvement. The family needed to make a decision.

"I'm not a kook, but when I called Father Roberto he told me all about you," Weymouth told me. "I watched the broadcast, several times. I was fascinated by the Mexican connection."

"That's what got all the attention."

"My mother didn't know I was looking. She accepts the doctors' advice."

"I think that's wise."

"I asked if she would just let me go to Mass. It was a moment of complete despair. God didn't speak to me at all. Then I walked out and saw you."

"Must have been a little spooky."

"It was an answer to my prayer."

"I'm in Oaxaca to visit a church Padre Roberto mentioned. Helping a young woman find her husband."

That didn't make much sense. He didn't seem interested.

"I went to Mass to find help and there you were," he said. "It's a pretty strong coincidence."

"It is."

"You don't see it as the will of God?"

I don't think God makes some guy dissatisfied in Durham so he'll go save somebody in Oaxaca. Makes him miss a flight so he'll be wandering around.

I tried to smile.

"Would you at least come to the hospital with me?" Weymouth said.

"I have to take care of this woman. She doesn't know where I am."

"It doesn't have to be now. Anytime you're free."

I'm afraid I'm terribly busy, from now until the end of time. What was I supposed to say to this guy?

"I'll help you with your work," he said. "I can make a substantial donation."

"We've got all the money we can handle, actually."

"I'll help you some other way. Anything. Help find this woman's husband. I just want to do everything I can. You must have a father."

Actually, I didn't. But I knew the feeling.

"If there's anything more to try, I want to do it," he said.

I sighed. "Let me call this young woman. See what she's doing."

I stepped out into the blinding sunlight. Didn't want to desecrate the place with a phone call.

This was definitely awkward. Forgot to mention it, Heather, but I'm a world-renowned faith healer.

"I'm fine," she said. "But I can't stand this sitting around. I want to go to the airport."

"The taxi guys will get in touch with us."

"They probably forgot already."

"Not when there's a reward."

Dolores had told me Mexican men would do anything for a little extra cash. "Why don't we go at seven o'clock?" I said. "Close to when the flight was due."

"Like he had the wrong night?"

"He might think you'd take the same flight the next day."

That was pretty feeble. I didn't want to spend hours out there. That was also the time when Juan Enrique's replacement would come on. We could speak to him.

"I'll come back around five," I said. "We'll make a decision."

The sun was blinding out there. Weymouth stood to one side as I called.

"Everything all right?" he said.

"It's fine. I told her I'd be back around five."

"We'll take a car from my hotel. I'll make sure you're back."

The hotel was just a couple of blocks away. We walked through the outdoor art gallery, past vendors of various kinds. Even the Mexicans seemed stunned by the heat. The men at the hotel entrance—bellboys and security guys—bustled around at Weymouth's approach. The car was a huge SUV. Not my choice, but I liked the air conditioning. I didn't envy the driver on those narrow streets.

"I appreciate this," Weymouth said. "Can't believe I ran into you." He seemed upbeat, much different from the slumping weeping man I saw in the church.

"Seems to be my karma these days."

Everywhere I turned, I met someone who needed healing.

The situation was hopeless. A massive stroke five days before, one side of his brain gone. But my own father had died of a heart attack when I was sixteen, and I'd always wondered if better care could have saved him. Weymouth had brought up the one thing that could make me come.

"This doesn't sound hopeful," I said.

"Except for the fact of finding you, which is incredible. I called my mother, and she said they're giving him adrenalin. They might have taken out the respirator by the time we get there."

I'd never been around a man who was close to death. My father had already died by the time I got to the hospital.

"Tell me again what brought you down here," Weymouth said. "I still can't believe it."

"To Oaxaca, specifically, there's a Virgin I want to see. Padre Roberto told me about it."

"The Virgin of Solitude. That's a Basilica across town. We'll pass a couple of blocks from there on our way."

That was it.

"It refers to Mary when Jesus was in the tomb," he said. "The Virgin of Guadalupe is special to all Mexico. But people in Oaxaca love the Virgin of Solitude."

I didn't understand all that.

"I decided in my early twenties I wanted to know all about the religion I was raised in," Weymouth said. "The Episcopal Church. Read theology like a law book, which was the other text I was perusing at the time. It didn't hold up under cross-examination."

It tends not to.

"When I got to Mexico years later I threw all that away. Attended Mass before I spoke Spanish. It might as well have been Latin. What I saw around me was pure love and devotion. I saw it better because I didn't know the words."

Exactly.

"I joined the church in that spirit. Didn't study or try to understand. Said yes to everything."

"They let you?"

"Down here. Never would have in the states. My Spanish is better now. I understand the words. But I don't pay much attention. Just give myself to the ritual."

This guy should practice Zen.

The traffic was horrendous. All the streets were one lane, and there was no wiggle room. Intersections were a disaster.

"I hope you're not worried about traffic," I said.

"They don't think my father will go right when they remove the respirator. They say he could last forty-eight hours."

"*Rain*," the driver said, pointing to some dark clouds. "*We'll have rain before long.*"

"There's a thunderstorm almost every day in the summer," Charles said. "Blows out of nowhere. Cools things off."

I looked forward to that.

We arrived at the hospital, which was on the other side of town. The place seemed tiny, more like a private clinic. There was plenty of staff around, and they looked competent.

He was Charles Sr., and the respirator was still in when I got there. I didn't know what he'd looked like in real life, but the respirator was huge, went down his throat, distorted his face. It looked horrible.

Mrs. Weymouth sat beside him. She was petite, heavy but also delicate, with silver hair. She moved slowly, seemed arthritic. She shook my hand.

"Charles let me watch that video earlier, just to pass the time," she said. "I can't believe he walked out of here and found you."

"Very strange."

"It's the Internet I can't get over. To watch you on that screen, then have you walk through the door."

That made even me feel a little weird.

A nurse suggested we move to a waiting room next door. We might not want to see them remove the respirator. It would take a few minutes.

Charles went to the bathroom. I sat down with Mrs. Weymouth.

"This has been horrible," she said.

"It must have."

"To come here after all these years and have this happen. I'm sure Charles would have had the stroke anyway. It was just bad timing."

"Yes."

"Charles Sr. and I are not Catholics."

"Your son told me."

"We haven't known what to make of it. It's just not like him. Like the art. I admire European painting. Landscapes and things. Everything Charles brings home is so garish. Violent and passionate."

A good description of Mexican art.

"He's a wonderful tax attorney. Handles money for wealthy people, including his father and me. I'm not sure what they'd think if they knew this side of him."

I nodded.

"What I'm trying to say is that my faith is important to me. But I'm not expecting a miracle."

"I'm not either."

"My husband is about to die."

"It certainly sounds that way."

"He wouldn't want to live if he couldn't speak or think."

"No."

"I don't think he's been conscious the whole five days we've been here. But a couple of hours ago, after Charles went to church, it did look as if his father woke up. I haven't told Charles."

I nodded.

"His breathing changed. Not the metronomic thing the machine produces. His eyes were open, though that's been true from time to time. I don't know that he sees anything. But there was a look of alarm in his eyes, a pleading look. Some might have seen a plea to live. I thought he wanted to die."

"He may."

"There are worse things than death. Living with that contraption in your mouth might be one of them."

The nurse came in after a few minutes and told us they'd removed it.

"His breathing is harsh at the moment," she said. Her English was perfect. "Like he's gasping for air. You might not want to come in, Mrs. Weymouth."

"How long will this go on?"

"Just a few minutes, we think." She looked at me. "The young Mr. Weymouth wanted you to come."

"That seems better," Mrs. Weymouth said. "You do whatever you do. Then I'll come in."

I had no idea what to do.

I walked into the small room. Charles was standing at his father's side, and I stepped to the other. The old man was wheezing, had a desperate look in his eyes. It reminded me of a dog I'd seen after it had been hit by a car. It looked startled and desperate, reduced to its animal nature.

"We're here, Dad," Charles said. "I'm here, and Mother is here. And a friend is here to help. We're with you."

The man looked better with that hardware removed. At the same time, he wore that expression of deep alarm, staring at the ceiling, gasping for air.

Charles touched his father's shoulder. I put one hand on the man's chest, another on his head.

"Do you feel anything?" Charles said.

"His chest is really working. He's in distress."

There was a computer screen above his head, a digital readout of his blood pressure and pulse, also his breathing rate. They were all high.

The nurse stepped in, looked at the monitor.

"He's struggling for breath," Charles said.

"That's normal at this point," she said. "Completely normal. I might give him more adrenaline."

"*More* adrenaline?"

"He's got to take over the breathing function. When he does, the breathing will calm down."

She came to my side of the bed, where the IV was, turned one of the knobs. She watched for a few moments, turned it back, stepped away.

"I'll keep checking," she said. "I know this is hard. But it's perfectly normal."

She stepped out of the room.

There was an icon of the Virgin above the bed, below the monitor.

"People who come to me pray to the Virgin," I said.

"I've been doing nothing else," Charles said. "Are you feeling anything?"

"Just this terrific struggle to breathe. It's a battle."

It didn't seem something that could last long. Either it would relax or shut down altogether.

There was a strong smell in the room. It was as if Mr. Weymouth were bringing it up from the depths of his lungs, as if there were poisons there.

I wondered if it was the smell of death.

A doctor stepped into the room, a bearded heavyset man. Charles seemed to know him. I wondered what he thought of me standing with my hands on his patient, but he didn't say anything.

"His breathing hasn't stabilized," he said, staring at the monitor. "It will come down." He too spoke excellent English.

He put his hand on Charles's back in a gesture of sympathy.

"Often we suggest people not be here for this," he said. "It's quite distressing."

"I want to be here for him," Charles said.

The doctor nodded, stepped out of the room.

There was nothing more for them to do. Their intervention was the respirator. The family had decided to remove it.

"Do you feel anything, Hank?" Charles said. "Is he coming back?"

All I'd felt was that terrific struggle in the man's chest, a machine laboring to perform. It seemed to diminish under my hand.

"I think the breathing is getting regular," I said. "It's calming down."

The nurse had stepped back in. The three of us watched the monitor.

"It's coming down," she said. "You can see it."

I watched the numbers with them, but under my hand something else happened.

"Or maybe it's stopping altogether," I said.

"Stopping?" Charles said.

I looked at the nurse. "I think his breathing has stopped. I don't feel it."

She came over and put her hand on his chest, beside mine. "We wouldn't have expected that so soon," she said.

"He's stopped breathing," I said. "You should get Mrs. Weymouth."

The nurse stepped out to get Charles's mother.

"You can't do anything?" Charles said. "You don't feel life?"

"He was struggling. Grasping at something he couldn't have. He gave up."

"You're letting him die."

"I'm not doing anything. It's what's happening."

Mrs. Weymouth came in. She stepped over and stood beside her son. He allowed her to move closer, toward the head of the bed.

She touched her hand to her husband's face. I took my hand from his head. There was a feeling of warmth there, above his head.

"I'm with you, darling," she said. "We're with you."

"I thought you could heal him," Charles said. "I thought you were sent for that."

"I wasn't sent," I said. "I've never healed anyone."

"It's time for him to go," Mrs. Weymouth said.

What seemed too bad was that Charles couldn't see the beauty of it. He was so fixated on healing that he couldn't see his father's relief from suffering.

It was understandable. Death was the last thing he wanted.

I'd never been with someone when he died. I'd seen Jake after he was long since dead, discovered the body. But I'd never watched an actual death.

It didn't seem sudden, the way it did in B-grade movies. I had felt him cease to breathe, and we'd seen that on the monitor. He gradually grew more still, more peaceful. He passed away. I'd always thought that was a euphemism, but it described exactly what happened. The man passed away, and his body was left.

Julie told me later that the warmth I'd felt at the crown of his head was the spirit passing. She'd felt that too, several times, one summer when she volunteered at an AIDS hospice.

We stood and watched, I don't know how long. Five minutes, ten? We stood and watched the man gradually grow more still and more peaceful.

Something in that was important to me. My father had his heart attack at work, and by the time we got to the hospital he was dead. We didn't even see the body; my mother thought it would be too upsetting. So in that most important moment of my life, I wasn't there. I didn't see it happen, wouldn't have been able to watch anyway, I was so young and scared. The whole thing was too much for me. My father just disappeared.

The first thing I had to do in practice, the first major task, was to absorb my father's death. In real life I'd suppressed it almost completely. For God knows how many *sesshins*—long retreats when such things came up—I had dealt with the sorrow of that, its unfinished nature. It seemed the sorrow would never end. Jake always said: it goes on as long as it has to. Let it happen.

Eventually I got to a place where I was reconciled to my father's death. But I wasn't reconciled to the fact of death, not until I saw Charles Weymouth Sr. die, a man I'd never known. It was natural and necessary, made way for more life.

What a thing to be present for. It was worth the whole trip to Mexico.

It's not that I don't believe in healing. If something I did when I touched Julie's breast caused healing energy to flow and kept cancer from taking her life, that was good. If I helped Jose's leg grow straighter, helped Hortensia conceive.

But I also feel that life as it is doesn't need healing, all of its sorrows, tragedies, difficulties, with death at the end. Life as it is, the whole process, is fine; it's marvelous. No one should interfere with that—or want to.

A feeling of peace spread over the whole room. At some point Charles said to his mother, "Is he dead now?"

She said, "Yes. He's dead."

He put his head on his father's chest and sobbed. She put her hand on his head and nodded to me. I touched my hand to his back. He needed to go through this. At least he was there for it and saw it.

I walked out the door and down the hall.

NINETEEN

The thunderstorm happened. It actually began while I was still in the hospital room, terrific claps of thunder, a torrential downpour. I'd never heard a storm begin quite that way. It was as if there were a huge cosmic bucket, and it turned over with a splat. The rain went on and on. The drops seemed huge.

I would not want to criticize the beautiful city of Oaxaca, but they didn't have much of a drainage system. It was the kind of storm where you think, "It'll be over soon, it can't rain that hard for long," but it went on and on, and water flowed down the street like a river. I saw a leather sandal go by, and a hubcap. It looked as if you could step into it and be swept away.

The driver from the hotel was standing in the vestibule, smoking a cigarette, watching.

"*Much rain,*" he said.

I nodded. "*El Señor died,*" I said.

He crossed himself. "*I'm sorry for your loss.*"

"*I didn't actually know him. Only his son.*"

It was impossible to explain what I was doing there.

"*The sky is weeping at the death,*" he said.

Eventually the rain slowed down, then finally stopped, quite suddenly.

"*Are you returning to the hotel?*" he said.

It was 4:15. I had some time.

"*I'd like to go to the Basilica.*"

"I can take you. The young señor said to take you back."

"I'd like to walk. Now that it's not raining. Is it far?"

"Five blocks down, two blocks over."

"I'd prefer to walk. Now that it's cool."

"If the rain begins again, I'll come and find you."

I thanked him and shook his hand, began walking.

The city seemed refreshed by the rain. Oaxaca in the summer had that weather pattern, as I would discover over the next week or so. The early morning was pleasantly cool, the shadows long, sometimes a slight mist around. As the sun came up it burned the mist and coolness away, and the midday sun—into the late afternoon—could be overwhelming. An afternoon thunderstorm—often quite violent—came as a relief. The evening would seem pleasantly washed out by the rain.

The streets were coming to life after the storm, hardly anyone around. I was glad I'd walked. This neighborhood was not at all like the area around Santo Domingo, not nearly as touristy, more like the shops townspeople might use. It seemed much more authentically Mexican. Though what would I know.

In the weeks of my life that began when I touched Julie's breast and included so much weird coincidence, so many claims of divine intervention, of miraculous healing—I never knew what to make of it all—there is only one moment that seemed like a true miracle to me, and it was about to happen as I walked through that part of the city. I realize that it doesn't compare in importance to a woman being cured of breast cancer or an infertile couple conceiving, but who knows if those things really happened? I was never convinced.

I walked the *cinque quadras* over and the *dos quadras* down to the Basilica of the Virgin of Solitude and came to a small outdoor stadium beside the basilica, just some bleachers beside the main courtyard of the church. A couple of days later I saw

a performance there, one that seemed vaguely religious, associated with the basilica. But on this Sunday, there was only one
person sitting in the stands, after the storm.

He hadn't sat through the storm; he wasn't soaked. I couldn't
imagine why he was there, though it was a good vantage point
for looking down on the basilica and the courtyard beyond it,
houses and businesses past that.

As I looked at him—his lean, strong body; his long, dark
hair, slicked back and glistening; his sideburns; his devilishly
handsome face—there was no doubt in my mind who it was.
The weird thing is that I think I knew even before I noticed
those things. It was as if he'd dropped out of heaven and landed
right there, so I couldn't miss him. As if the Virgin stepped out
of the basilica and said, "Hey stupid, doesn't this look like a
Mexican Elvis?"

"Patricio," I said.

"*Yes.*"

It looked like I'd get the reward. I wondered what I'd spend
it on.

"*I've been taking care of Heather and your son. We got into
town this morning.*"

"This morning? I thought she would get here last night."

"*Our flight from Dallas to Mexico City was delayed. We missed
the flight to Oaxaca.*"

Those words didn't seem to penetrate. He hadn't done much
air travel.

"But how did you come this morning?"

"*They put us on the next flight. It was at seven this morning.*"

"How could that be? The flight was last night."

He just didn't get it.

"*I thought she would come tonight,*" he said. "*If she came at all.*"

"*What did you do last night?*"

This whole conversation had an eerie feel to it, as if there were nothing more likely than that we would run into each other and start talking this way. It was weirdly matter of fact.

"I stayed at the airport for a long time, hoping there was some mistake. Then a man gave me a ride into town. He said you never know when the airplanes will work. Half the time they don't. I came to this church, which is the one place in the city where my family sometimes comes. I got my food at the stalls."

There were a number of food stalls in the courtyard in front of us. *"I slept last night on this bench. I spent the day praying to the Virgin, hoping that my wife and child would come tonight. I attended Mass I don't know how many times. Just now I was saying one last prayer before I took a bus to the airport. If I didn't find Heather at the airport tonight I didn't know what I would do. It's a miracle that you found me like this. It's the answer to all my prayers."*

It was a miracle, I agreed. The one Mexican in Oaxaca— maybe the world—who looked like Elvis. I just happened to run into him.

"What if you had not walked by at this very moment?" he said.

Well, the taxistas at the airport would have been all over him. They had probably asked every skinny Mexican they saw that day if his name was Patricio. Or Juan Enrique would have seen him. His sleepy Mexican eyes seemed to pick up everything. If all that failed, Heather and I were planning to go to the airport. Something would have worked out.

"Why were you walking by here at this moment?" he said.

"I was trying to help a man who was very sick, in a hospital. But he died."

"I'm sorry the man died. But I'm glad you walked along."

"Maybe he died so I could come here." I didn't believe that for a minute, but it seemed like something to say.

"He might have died to answer my prayers. We should thank the Virgin together."

"We should."

He crossed himself and said some words in his native language. I assume the Virgin is multilingual. His language did include a number of clicks. Some of the clicks bled over into his Spanish.

"*I'm sorry,*" he said. "*I should have prayed in Spanish.*"

"*It's all right. I was praying in English.*"

That was the language the Virgin might have trouble with.

"*Do you know where the restaurant La Olla is?*" I said.

"*I only know the churches here.*"

"*You know Santo Domingo?*"

"*Of course. The church with all the gold, where the rich people go. But they don't have our Virgin.*"

"*Heather is staying at a small hotel near Santo Domingo.*" I didn't think I'd introduce him to the concept of a B&B. "*It's behind a restaurant named La Olla. Wait. I haven't been thinking. You can talk to Heather.*"

She was just a phone call away. Though she said they didn't do well on the phone.

I dialed the number and handed him the phone.

"Heather," he said. "This is Patricio." He didn't start to cry, but tears poured from his eyes, while he had a big smile on his face. She said some words. "I'm with a man who found me here. At the church."

"Hank," I said.

"A man named Hank. He's with me now. We're very close to you. I can walk there."

"Let me speak to her, Patricio."

He handed me the phone.

"I'll put him in a cab, Heather. I'll send him to the restaurant. He'll be there in ten minutes."

"How did you find him?"

"I just stumbled across him. He was sitting in these bleachers beside the church. He looked just like you said. Like Elvis."

A hunka hunka burnin' love.

"I was getting more and more depressed," she said. "I thought we'd never find him."

"It's a miracle."

They were becoming commonplace in my life.

"He'll be there in ten minutes. You can walk out and wait in front of the restaurant."

"I've got to change the baby. Make him ready."

"Don't worry, Heather. His father will wait."

I gave the phone back to Patricio.

"I will see you soon, Heather. Kiss my boy for me."

I didn't think his English was that bad. A hell of a lot better than Heather's Spanish.

There was a part of me that would have loved to be there for that reunion. There was another part that figured the nicest thing I could do was not be there. I'd only be in the way.

"*What are your plans now?*" I said.

"*There is a bus that leaves at 11:00 for my village. We will be on that.*"

"*Heather may be tired.*"

"*We can sleep on the bus. We thought this would be best for our son, since he can sleep. My family thought we would arrive this morning. We need to get home.*"

"*If you change your mind, there is a bed in the hotel. You can stay there tonight.*"

"*Thank you, señor.*"

As it turned out, they were gone when I got back.

"*Also, I'm planning to stay at the church for several hours. I'll have dinner at a restaurant in town. I won't be back for some time. It's fine to use the room.*"

"*Thank you, señor.*"

"*There's a door that you can close.*"

"*Thank you.*"

230

I didn't see how I could make it any plainer. I took out my wallet. *"I want to give a present to you and Heather. I'd like to pay for dinner for you at the restaurant in front of the hotel."*

"That isn't necessary."

"I'd like to do it. In celebration of your son."

I could always come up with some excuse. I gave him 400 pesos.

"This is too much for dinner."

"The restaurant is expensive. I want to make sure you have enough." Heather would probably have a rib eye.

"I appreciate this, señor."

"It's a gift for you and your son."

Just in case he really is Jesus Christ.

We began walking toward the street corner.

"I met Heather on the airplane from Dallas," I said. *"A woman who sat beside me told me I had to take care of her until she found her husband. She said it was like Mary with the baby Jesus."*

"She is like Mary."

This guy was in love.

"Her father also asked me, by phone, if I would care for his daughter."

"Her father is a strange man."

"But he loves his daughter. And respects you very much."

"He does love his daughter."

He wasn't sure about the other point.

"Perhaps our paths will cross in the United States," I said.

"I hope that will happen."

It didn't seem likely, but what the hell.

"As a last gift for your son, I'm going to pay for the taxi that will take you to him."

"I can easily walk. It isn't far."

"The taxi will know where to go."

I didn't want to leave anything up to chance.

I hailed a taxi, put Patricio in the back.

"Do you know the restaurant La Olla?" I said to the driver.

"Of course. Every taxi driver knows this restaurant."

"How much?" Dolores had told me to get the price first thing. He considered this important question. *"Six?"*

I could have probably gotten him down to four, but what was the point?

"For your trouble, señor." I gave him eight.

"Gracias."

"Adios, Patricio." We shook hands. He wore a big smile.

The taxi took off like a bat out of hell.

And I walked back to the corner, and down the steps, to enter the basilica.

*

The legend went that, early in the seventeenth century, a peasant was entering Oaxaca with a mule train when he noticed a mule at the end that wasn't his, carrying a crate on its back. He didn't know how or where he had acquired it. When he tried to separate it from his mules it wouldn't budge. Finally he got more forceful with it, and the mule dropped dead on the spot, right at the site of the present-day basilica.

No one in the community had any idea who the mule belonged to, but when they opened the crate they found an image of the Virgin, which seemed to be comforting an image of Jesus. It came to be seen as the patron saint of Oaxaca, also of mariners, many of whom walked on pilgrimage to see it. The basilica was built to house the image, clothed in black velvet and topped by a golden jeweled crown, high above the altar.

It remained an active church, with a large congregation of local—mostly, it seemed—poor people. At the side door where

I entered—the massive rear doors had been closed against the storm—an old woman in tatters stood barefoot, begging. Further in, a young blind man held a cup.

Two Masses were celebrated that evening, one in honor of a young woman's *quince años*, the other celebrating the fiftieth anniversary of a couple's marriage (the woman was dressed as a bride and carried a bouquet). Different priests celebrated the two Masses; otherwise, I might not have known when one ended and the other began. Mass just seemed to go on and on.

Many people just sat in the basilica, not celebrating one Mass or another. That was something I would notice throughout my stay in Oaxaca: There were always people in the basilica.

I knew it was the place I'd been looking for as soon as I stepped in. It wasn't as magnificent as Santo Domingo, but it was definitely vast. The architecture was similarly Baroque, with carvings and artwork all over the place. It would have taken days really to see it all, and I did spend days perusing it in the coming week.

But I wasn't there for the art or the magnificence of the building. I was there for the people. And the people were there for that image of the Virgin that hung above the altar, at the center of everything—that strange, ornate image, wrapped in a black velvet cloak and topped with a crown, holding out her hands as if in comfort.

I sat far down in the front, in the second row (just like Julie), so I could see her.

It wasn't much different from Mass in Durham. Many people just sat there, looking around, as if they experienced something just through their presence. I didn't understand most of what was going on, though I had gotten to the point where I followed the general outlines. Still I was the object of considerable attention, as the whole crowd stared at me, the only gringo, as far as I could tell, in the building that day, at least the only one actually participating.

The music was uninspired, though the group around me sang in a spirited way, especially a developmentally disabled young man who was extremely loud and terribly off key. I tried and failed to understand the homily, though I called on my best Spanish, and worked at it. The priest lost me after about three sentences.

There was a perceptible shift in attention when it was time for the sacrament, and we knelt for the confessional prayer before it. Still the most moving moment in Mass was when the priest held up the Host as if to offer it, and that ragged crowd of people—the forgotten and bedraggled poor—came up to receive it. I sat in wonder. It was what I had come to see.

Finally, after two days of struggle, I seemed to have arrived in Mexico, and to have found what I was looking for.

It was the same thing I'd already seen back in Durham, the first time I went to Mass.

*

One of the greatest pieces of religious scripture in the world is a two-page letter that the Zen teacher Eihei Dogen wrote to a layperson in the first half of the thirteenth century. I've never heard why he wrote the letter, or who the layperson was, whether he had asked some question. But in that offhanded piece of writing, not an official document at all, Dogen summed up all his teaching, and all the teaching of the Buddha. Eventually it was gathered as the first fascicle of his great life's work, the *Shobogenzo*.

The first time I read it—chanted it, actually—I was just starting to sit with Jake, didn't know a thing about Buddhism, and the hairs on the back of my neck stood up. It was nevertheless years before I understood any of it, including the knotty opening passage:

As all things are buddha-dharma, there are delusion, realization, practice, birth and death, buddhas and sentient beings. As myriad things are without an abiding self, there is no delusion, no realization, no buddha, no sentient being, no birth and death. The buddha way, in essence, is leaping clear of abundance and lack; thus there are birth and death, delusion and realization, sentient beings and buddhas. Yet in attachment, blossoms fall—and in aversion, weeds spread.

*

What he was saying, I think, was that on the one hand there is common reality, the world as we all see it and try to make sense of it. On the other hand, to the eye of realization, none of these things actually exists: there is only vast emptiness, where no single thing has any existence at all. But after all your practicing and striving to understand that, once you finally see it, there sits the world as it was before, with all those things in it. And whether you've seen it or not, the things you love die and the things you hate keep springing up.

That last sentence is the real kicker: Now deal with the world as it is, big boy.

In my life, it seemed that I had tried to understand religion—understand who I was—by reading about it and pondering it. I just about burst a blood vessel reading Christianity and trying to make it my own. I was like Charles Weymouth when he tried to find it that way.

Then I met Jake, this little Jewish guy, the most ordinary human being in the world, who said, "Don't do that, just sit and stare at the wall, look into yourself: everything is there. You don't need scriptures. You don't need words. Just sit and look into yourself."

I found that to be true. It was the most miraculous thing I ever discovered, and I am eternally grateful to that practice, and to the little guy who showed it to me. I found the mystical heart of all religion, and I'm still finding it, there's no end to it. It's right here, and it goes on and on.

Jesus is the Son of God and the Virgin Mary is his mother.

Or there is one God and his name is Allah.

Except when his name is Yahweh.

And of course, all things are Brahman, which has no beginning and no end.

Except that the Dao that can be named is not the true Dao.

And no matter what you believe, no matter what religion you follow, flowers die when you love them and weeds spread when you hate them. The father you love dies, and the people you can't stand keep popping out of the woodwork, talking on their cellphones.

I had come to Mexico to find the true Virgin, the heart of healing. People told me I had the power of healing myself, but I didn't see how that was possible. Now I had found her, though she didn't look the way I had expected (and though that other Virgin was also real, even when she was back in Durham).

And no matter where you found her, or didn't find her, here were human beings, still suffering.

In many ways all I did in the Basilica was sit zazen. I sat there in full awareness, with that wonderful smell of Mexico all around, the gutters pouring and dripping outside, people all around me groaning and singing off key, the priest up front speaking those incomprehensible words. It had been a long day, including an early departure, that endless wait for luggage in the airport, the husband who never showed up, the weeping wife, a long walk through the glaring sun, a disappointing visit to church, an unlikely encounter with a grief-stricken son, a father's agonizing death, the unlikely discovery of the husband, the happy reunion which I assumed took place. It had been a long day, almost endless, and now I'd sat through Mass twice on these hard pews, but I was happy, I was positively joyful, I was giddy with happiness. I could have stayed forever.

The first Mass—the quince años celebration—was led by a most distinguished man in beautiful vestments, roughly my age. People obviously worshiped the ground he walked on, and the homily he gave—though I myself couldn't understand it—seemed well organized and beautifully delivered. The second—the celebration of the fiftieth anniversary—was conducted by a little man who was so old he couldn't even stand, but had to sit on a stool. Maybe he was the priest who married the couple in the first place. He muttered his way through the whole thing, seemed to conk out a couple of times, and when he gave the homily spoke away from the microphone so I couldn't even hear the words, though I wouldn't have understood them anyway.

During the first Mass, I went forward for the Eucharist with my arms crossed in front of me and the priest gave his blessing, Father, Son, Holy Spirit, making the sign of the cross on my forehead. But during the second, though I'd never heard of anyone taking the Eucharist twice (though I wasn't actually taking it), I went forward again with my arms crossed in front of me, but the old priest didn't seem to understand (or was he the only one who did understand?). He dunked the Host into the wine and popped it into my mouth.

I wasn't even Catholic! I hadn't gone to confession! I had never gone to confession! This ancient priest had put the Host into my mouth! What was I to do? *There's* a Zen koan for you.

I chewed up the body and blood of our Sacred Lord Jesus Christ and swallowed it.

I started to cry when I got back to the pew, not just in reaction to the Host, but because I finally belonged, I was a part of things. I wasn't a clueless gringo. People weren't even staring at me anymore. I was part of the human race.

Tears were flowing, but a tremendous glow spread all through me. And at that moment, a disabled girl with a horrible limp hobbled by, holding her mother's hand. She seemed to stumble, and I took her hand, touched it, and held it. The glow spread right into her. A radiant smile came over her face, a look of astonishment, as if someone had slapped her, as if suddenly she recognized me. She stared at me, eyes wide with delight, couldn't seem to stop staring. She gripped my hand. She didn't want to let go.

"Mama," she said, tugging at her mother's hand. "Oh! Mama!"

About the Author

Pittsburgh native David Guy is the author of five previous novels, including *The Autobiography of My Body* and *Jake Fades*, and one nonfiction book, *The Red Thread of Passion: Spirituality and the Paradox of Sex*. He also wrote two books with his meditation teacher Larry Rosenberg, *Breath by Breath* and *Living in the Light of Death*. Guy taught for many years at his alma mater, Duke University, and now divides his time between his two favorite North Carolina cities, Durham and Asheville. **davidguy.org.**